the
house
with the blue
front door

ELIZABETH
BROMKE

ABOUT THIS BOOK

Beverly Castle lost her family, but she refuses to lose hope. Ready to distract herself from the heartache, Beverly returns to the newspaper where she works as a journalist. There, she asks her boss for permission to follow a scandalous lead related to the local high school. He agrees, as long as Beverly is able to separate work from her personal life. After all, in a small town, scandals are contagious.

Annette Best is just weeks away from completing a property exchange. Finances have forced her to trade out her gorgeous white colonial for a smaller red cottage around the corner. But to make the transaction, she must first clear the cobwebs from the old family home...and since she's at the mercy of her workaholic husband and distracted teen son, it's on

Annette to make sure no skeletons are left in any of the closets.

Jude Banks was able to shake her ex loose, thanks in part to a new job at the high school. Now, she wants life to slow down a little. That's when her neighbor shows up at her classroom on a mission to expose the truth about one of the former teachers...*and* about Harbor Hills.

Quinn Whittle is gainfully employed, her daughter is registered at Hills High, and their new house is starting to feel like home...until her neighbors call a meeting of the minds down by the mailboxes. Whereas Quinn has settled in, now the other three women's façades are starting to crack.

Welcome to Harbor Hills, Michigan, where neighbors are friends, and secrets spill across property lines. *The House with the Blue Front Door* is book two in this saga.

NOTE TO THE READER

Welcome to Harbor Hills! I'm so happy you're here. You're about to begin the second book in the Harbor Hills saga. Although this story can stand on its own, you may want to consider reading book one, *The House on Apple Hill Lane*, first, in order to avoid spoilers for that story and get to know the characters.

If you've already read *Apple Hill* or are ready to continue, here is a brief synopsis to remind you where the ladies are at the start of this story.

Quinn Whittle has moved into 696 Apple Hill Lane. A former hoarder's residence, it's been quite the job. Thanks to her new neighbors—and friends—she gets the place cleaned up. Not only has her house come together, but so, too, has her relationship with her daughter, Vivi. Thanks to a new mother-daughter bond, Vivi has chosen to live with Quinn in Harbor Hills. But the drama with the teen girl and her neighbor friend, Elijah, has only begun. Luckily, Quinn has her new job at the *Harbor Herald*, where her handsome boss, Forrest, keeps her busy.

Jude Banks has recently divorced Gene Carmichael. She's earned a spot teaching English at Hills High and is still a bit shy around her new neighbor friends. Nonetheless, Jude cares deeply for the newly developed connections on her street. But it's not just the other women or her job that serve to keep her content. She's decided to renovate her house, and there happens to be a handsome local who's just right for the job.

Annette Best and her husband, Roman, have decided to sell their house. They might already have a buyer, assuming everything goes well with the final inspection. Elijah, their teen son, is a big help...when he's not out cavorting with the neighbor girl or digging into the odd history of the house next door.

Beverly Castle lost her husband and daughter in a tragic car accident nearly one year ago. She's a broken woman, but she's a survivor, too. Up to now, she's been taking time off from her job at the newspaper. But going back to the office will help her move on. So long as her boss—a relative—lets her pursue the story she most desperately wants to write: the *truth* about what happened to her family on that fateful winter night.

The unnamed girl from the prologue left for school at her grandparents' behest. There remains little known about who she is and what her purpose to the greater story might be.

Happy reading!

Yours,
Elizabeth Bromke

PROLOGUE

I t had been a couple of years since the girl first arrived at 696 Apple Hill Lane. A couple of years since the car accident. A couple of years since she'd turned into an orphan twice over.

Once, when her mom and dad died in the accident. Twice, when her grandparents shipped her down to a boarding school for girls.

Living away from any and all family was hard, of course. It was made somehow easier *and* harder when she began receiving the letters.

Letters from Grandad.

Each one in his familiar, stilted capital letters on blank cream pages with ragged edges, like they were torn from a notebook. Money would appear here and there, tucked inside of the rough paper like a secret.

It was the girl's job to manage her tuition and room and board with the money. She hated this responsibility. It choked her like a too-big-bite of hot dog. She'd much rather not be in charge of herself. She'd rather be, well, just a girl.

At holidays, the girl found cards in her post, rather than letters. Sometimes, they were used. Grandad would scratch out greetings to him and Nana and signatures from strangers so they'd read like the cards inside library books.

~~*Dear Bernie and Irma,*~~
   KID:
   May blessings find you this season and always.
   ~~*Good tidings to you!*~~
   MERRY XMAS
   ~~*Bob and Rita Choldham*~~
   GRANDAD AND NANA

SHE WASN'T sure what she hated more about the notes. That Grandad called her *Kid* or that Nana never once signed them.

No, the girl had never received a letter from Nana. Just from Grandad. It was as if Nana had a grudge against the girl, though she couldn't possibly have known why. She couldn't possibly have known if it had to do with the death of Nana's daughter. Of the girl's mother. The girl couldn't know that, while losing one's own mother was awful, losing one's own daughter could be worse.

By the time the girl moved into her high school years, Nana got sick something terrible. So terrible that Grandad shuttled her up to the hospital at the university in Detroit.

The girl didn't want to go to Detroit, but that didn't matter. She wasn't invited. She was to stay at school. This suited her just fine, mostly.

Then, Nana took a turn.

This became evident in a letter, hand-addressed and handwritten to the girl at school. It rested in the wooden slot outside her dorm-room door, where other mail went, with little fanfare. But when she slid a finger beneath the lip of the envelope and worked it open, she was caught off guard.

Within the otherwise bland envelope awaited a cream page of *stationery*. At the top of the letterhead, an embossed *T*. Not *C* for Carlson. *T*. For...?

What struck the girl as especially strange was

how this small detail, this one sheet of customized paper, was entirely foreign to her. She hadn't the faintest that Grandad and Nana kept stationery. And if they had, she'd never have expected something so ornate. Grand. Expensive looking. And who was the *T*? Grandad's given name was Bernard. Nana's, Irma. And they were simple sorts, as she knew well. Then again, the girl also knew they owned more property than just 696. They owned the whole of the central east side of Harbor Hills, where Apple Hill Lane sat. An undeveloped community of would-be home-steads. Or something.

Despite their land ownership, though, the letter-head stood apart.

Even the message in the note—that Nana was officially dead—meant less to the girl than the peculiar stationery, which she'd later feel sore over. Sore. Regretful. Ugly.

KID:

IRMA PASSED. NO PUBLIC SERVICE. WILL HANDLE ALL AFFAIRS IN H.H. THEN WILL RETURN TO THE CITY. GOOD LUCK, KID.

GRANDAD (BERNIE)

· · ·

AFTER THE LETTER, Grandad would keep his word and stay on in Detroit for some years. So long, in fact, that she'd left and gone off to college by the time she'd sent a letter of her own. This one on plain notebook paper. A white page with cerulean blue lines underpinning her brief note. First, she'd wanted to know where he was. After that, how he was. Finally, when he'd go home.

The girl heard back from him on that same, special stationery. The lettering was the same stilted capitals as from years before. But this time, they carried new weight in them.

KID:

DETROIT'S IN THE REARVIEW. STARTED OVER. BACK ON APPLE HILL. COME SOON. NEED YOUR HELP WITH A <u>PRIVATE</u> MATTER.

GRANDAD HAD A SECRET.

And he was going to share it with the girl.

CHAPTER 1—BEVERLY

Beverly Castle stood at the entrance to the Harbor Hills cemetery, which just so happened to face Hills High.

She wasn't there for the graveyard, though. Not this time.

It was a cruel thing, to build a school across from a cemetery. Or vice versa. She glanced at the street sign, which stood like a scarecrow just yards away. Tugging her brown leather messenger bag closer to her body, she read the name. Schoolhouse Street. This was no chicken-or-the-egg conundrum. Clear as day, the school was here first. Made no sense to her why anyone, old-timey or not, would come along and decide it was a good idea to throw down rows of headstones just yards away from schoolchildren.

This was the first time Beverly had had such a thought. On previous trips—either to the school or to the cemetery—she'd been too distracted to think up the question. Making a mental note to follow up one day—endless potential stories knocked around in her head—she sucked in a deep breath and let it out to the count of five. Coping strategy. It didn't help.

Sunlight shone down brightly, and thick, late-summer humidity relaxed her loose waves into a limp sheet of brown hair. August in Harbor Hills was no different from July. Except for its proximity to fall, of course.

School would begin in just weeks. By then, Beverly knew she wouldn't have the nerve to enter the double doors. The same ones Kayla had stalked through for the one-and-only year of her high school career.

Beverly sealed her lips into a thin line and shifted in her boots. Even if it was hot and sticky, August didn't feel much like summer anymore. At least, not to Beverly. For that reason, she'd opted for black boots. Sensible ones that hit just below her knees and boasted modest, square heels. Jeans that hadn't fit the year before now hung loose at her waist and disappeared into the leather sheaths of the boots. She'd used one of Tom's belts to keep the jeans in place. On top, Beverly wore an airy blue blouse. That way she wouldn't sweat too much once inside.

A car passed by, too fast and too red, and Beverly found herself uselessly annoyed. With the world, but also with herself. She left her car in the gravel parking lot of the cemetery and crossed the street. The gravel lot was a straighter shot to the front office than if she'd parked in the visitor spots at the south end of the school building. At least, this is what Beverly told herself.

She came to Hills High on assignment. A piece for the paper. Teacher Turnover at Hills High. But another, more comfortable story sat on her very own street, just three houses up.

Even so, she'd promised her boss she'd come. She'd interview Principal Darry Ruthenberg, and she'd promise to keep things *upbeat*. Then, she'd get out of the school and would never go back there. Not ever again.

CHAPTER 2—ANNETTE

Annette Best plucked a champagne flute from her china cabinet and stuffed a dry cloth inside, rubbing the glass until it squeaked. She held it up to the kitchen window, allowing light in. Clean as a whistle.

That afternoon, she'd host what could very well be her last event in the Apple Hill house. A back-to-school meeting for the PTSO of Hills High. Champagne flutes and good china were overmuch. And really, it was hardly appropriate to serve mimosas at any school-related event. Still, Annette felt like she needed to elevate this particular one. Not to make fun. It wouldn't be fun, no. It was an obligation. Something required of the president: an annual event to drag new victims into the fold and remind the current members they were still hostage to the organization. She had to elevate this event so that the Hills High PTSO was a safe harbor in the recent storm of school drama and tragedy.

But not all the mimosas in the world would change that this meeting would take on an added degree of awkwardness. One particular mother would not be in attendance. And not for lack of an invitation, either. Then again, Beverly Castle wasn't about to fall prey to that sort of cruelty. Annette was no idiot.

At least Beverly hadn't ever served on the PTSO. For all Annette knew, she'd be none the wiser to the intimate gathering. That was the goal.

Annette had given serious consideration to hosting somewhere else, even going as far as propositioning other members. No one was willing. By the time she'd asked five mothers, they were a week out from the event, and no venue in town had an opening for that Friday night.

This was the moment when Annette reached out to Quinn, who presently helped clean flutes and the good china—stuff Annette had nearly forgotten she owned. She only had it out because she'd slowly— very slowly—begun packing the house.

"Were you on the PTSO at Vivi's old school?"

Annette asked innocently, forgetting herself for a
moment.

"Birch Harbor? Or St. Mary's?"

"Sorry." Annette winced. "I forgot. You have a
different story than most." She caught a hard expression on Quinn's face. "I don't mean that in a bad
way."

At this, Quinn rolled her eyes openly. "It's not a
good thing that my daughter didn't live with me for
two years."

"If you ask me, it's healthy." Annette meant every
word. "Seriously." She held her neighbor-friend's
gaze.

Quinn broke eye contact first. "How could
that be?"

"When I was a girl, I'd have died to get away
from my mom for a year."

Frowning, Quinn set down one gold-trimmed
plate and picked up another, running her damp
cloth slowly over its face. "Oh, please," she snorted.

Annette pursed her lips. "We didn't get along.
There were several rough years. We could have used
a break."

Quinn seemed to consider this, but there was no
chance to see the conversation through. Two sets of
footsteps trampled down the staircase.

Elijah and Vivi.

"Hi, you two!" Annette beamed. "Get your puzzle done?"

In the past few weeks, the two had forged an unlikely and fervent bond, spending every day together. Turning from strangers to best friends.

Were they more than friends?

Who could say? Teenagers were going to be teenagers, and Annette had accepted she'd fall far outside of the loop once Elijah started exploring young romance.

"Yep!" Vivi, it turned out, was somehow more comfortable than Elijah in his own house. She enjoyed paying visits to Annette, too, sometimes. Annette knew that eventually, Vivi would be the one to spill the beans. If there were beans to be spilled.

"We aren't hanging around for Moms' Night In," Elijah added, a wry smile on his mouth.

"And where do you *think* you're going, then?" Quinn asked, the recent drama of Vivi's runaway day still etched in lines on her forehead, Annette noticed.

"The backyard," Vivi groaned. It was a good-natured groan, though. If groans could be good-natured.

Quinn and Annette exchanged a brief, knowing look.

Annette cleared her throat. "What are you going to do out there?"

Elijah visibly reddened. Glaring hard at her, he mouthed *Stop*, plain as day.

Vivi was none the wiser, and her own reply relieved Annette and likely Quinn, too. "I told Eli I'd help him take down the fort."

"Oh," Annette replied, nodding. She looked at Quinn. "I told Elijah that we can't very well list a house with a poorly built wooden hovel out back. They'll think it's haunted or something." She chuckled.

Quinn smiled and seemed to relax. "Right, well, be careful."

Annette agreed. "Yes. The number of rusty nails protruding from that thing could fuel a town-wide tetanus outbreak." She laughed again at her own joke, but Quinn must have found it less funny.

"Seriously, Viv. Be careful."

Annette waved the two teens off and cocked her head at Quinn. "She isn't a kid, you know." It was bold, to offer a reminder like that. But they'd grown close, Quinn and Annette. As close as two neighbors could be. Closer than Annette was to Jude or Beverly, that was for sure.

Quinn finished polishing the last plate, lowered into a chair, and took a sip of her glass of water. "I forget that, actually."

With everything about set, Annette joined her, sitting adjacent, and stole a drink from her own glass —lemonade, always. "A lot of people look at teenagers and say the opposite. They say *they're just kids*. I disagree. And when parents treat their teenagers like children, that's when the problems start." Her eyes flashed to Quinn. "I don't mean that you do that. I think you give her a wide berth. Vivi is independent. I just mean—"

"You mean it as a reminder. I know. Trust her to make good decisions." Quinn looked thoughtful for a moment, swallowing another bite of watermelon. "Has Elijah ever done something stupid?"

Annette laughed. "Of course he has. All the time. Just like me. Just like Roman. Just like you." She dipped her chin and raised her eyebrows at Quinn. "Who doesn't screw up? It's human to screw up."

"Some stupid things cost more than others, though," Quinn pointed out.

A naked silence stilled the women. Neither looked at the other for a moment.

Annette gathered what Quinn implied. Kayla Castle. The fifteen-year-old who never would turn sixteen. Who'd never make another mistake. Not now. Not never. And the mother she left behind.

"Does she know about this?" Quinn asked, circling her finger around the table as if to suggest the get-together.

At that, Annette let out the breath she'd been holding. "I don't know, but I do know that she's at work today." Her mouth twisted sadly. "Which is for the best."

"How does she do it?" Quinn whispered.

Annette's frown deepened. "You mean cope?"

Quinn nodded.

"Honestly, I don't think she *is* coping."

CHAPTER 3—BEVERLY

"Beverly Castle for Mr. Ruthenberg," Beverly relayed to the school secretary, looking everywhere except the woman's eyes. Eye contact had become brutal.

Beverly was *that* one in town. The one people made sad eyes at. Cooed over. Clicked their tongues about and crossed themselves for. Some were better than others. Elaine Sutton, secretary of Hills High, was one of the worst.

"Oh, Mrs. Castle," Elaine whimpered. "He just went to the cafeteria to check on the back-to-school breakfast for faculty and staff. He'll be here any minute." She shook her head. "I am *so* sorry."

There it was. The apology. This time hidden in a separate woe—her boss's tardiness.

Beverly tried to focus the line of conversation on Darry. Pin Elaine there and keep her focused and keep everyone from crying. Yes, people sometimes did cry for her. "If he's late to our meeting, then I guess he'll have to serve lunch detention," Beverly joked.

Elaine knitted her eyebrows together. "Oh. That's typically reserved for students—"

"There you are!" Darry Ruthenberg's voice boomed from behind Beverly. "I was about to write you up for ditching."

"Nice try. I'll make the jokes around here," Beverly shot back, surprising even herself at how easy it came. The banter. The comfort. The back-and-forth. Her smile slipped away, and she added, "You're the one who's late."

He loosened his tie and waved her his way—in the opposite direction of his office and toward the front doors.

Beverly hooked a thumb over her shoulder. "Wouldn't it be better to meet—?"

"Anywhere but here," he replied. "In fact, I was going to call you and ask if we could do this somewhere else." There was no tone to his words. They came out matter-of-factly. Like *he* was the one who felt a stifling suffocation within the four walls of

Hills High. Like her own tragedy had nothing to do with it.

Soon enough, they were seated at a window table at Eat Street, a cheesy diner that had been around as long as Beverly could remember.

After they each put in an order for coffee, Darry stretched back in his vinyl-padded chair. "Okay, so," he began, starting so she didn't have to, "first of all, *turnover* is sort of...a bad word."

"I know," Beverly answered, suddenly finding herself more rapt with the story than she previously had.

"*Turnover* suggests—"

She finished his sentence for him. "That teachers are scrambling to get out of there."

"And they aren't." He anchored his forearms on the table and leaned toward her. "Look, Bev."

Smirking at the nickname, she cocked her head, as if he might change her mind.

"We lost some teachers over the summer. Two support staff. One admin—my dean."

"Right," she replied, her notebook still a fresh white page in front of her. She'd already gotten the basics before this meeting.

"Two teachers retired. One support staff had

health issues." He held his hands up. That was it. Case solved.

Not so fast. "Some people think the pay is low. That's what I've heard."

"All teacher pay is low. Across America," he shot back. "But ours is higher than average for the county *and* the state. Look at Detroit's numbers. You'll see what I mean."

"Some people say we're top heavy." She inwardly cringed at her choice of *we're*. As if she were still connected. She wasn't.

"We aren't replacing the dean. And off the record? That was a political decision, by the way." He hadn't waited for her to agree to keep such a morsel *off the record*.

She would, though.

"Okay, so you've accounted for four positions. What about the others?"

"Right. Support staff is never a sure thing. They're paid minimum wage. No benefits. Standard protocol. Again, you can cross-check me there. The second aide who left had no ties to the area. Single young woman. She wanted to settle down. Hadn't found a guy. You know how that goes."

Beverly didn't. Not exactly. She made a note, and when she looked back up, Darry's eyes had fallen to her page. He blew out a sigh and ran one hand through his hair—thick hair that he'd blown up and back in a dated, early-nineties way. And yet, it wasn't unappealing...

"So, of the other six teachers, one was another young lady. Looking to settle down. Again, no ties. She'd come to us from a different suburb. And one before that. Bounced around a lot."

"And you hired her?"

"She was good," Darry reasoned, pressing on. "Two others decided to leave the profession altogether—which might sound juicy, but it's not. Teaching is hard work. Public education has gone through growing pains in the country over the past couple of decades. Heck, since forever."

Beverly folded her arms across her chest. She was getting nowhere. "We're down to three."

He gave her a look, something soft but unyielding. Their coffee arrived, and the waitress didn't linger. Beverly kept her gaze on Darry, and he kept his on her. "Why are you doing this story, Bev?"

"Taxpayers want to know about the school. The inner workings. Behind the scenes. It's hot."

His jaw set. "You know about the other three, Bev."

She narrowed her stare, only just. Swallowed as

discreetly as she could. "I know about *one*. *One* Hills High teacher, Darry."

He shook his head and rapped his hands on the table, breaking their eye lock and fixing his coffee up with sugar and creamer. Too much of both. "The other two were a married couple. Moved out of town."

She was close. So close. "You haven't updated the website, you know."

Darry flashed his eyes up. "Huh?"

"The website. If it's Mr. and Mrs. Spectre who're leaving, well, they're still listed as current faculty."

He fidgeted, pretending he needed even more sugar and taking a moment to add another packet. "Right, we need to update."

"So, it *is* them?"

Darry looked up, his sugar packet hovering above the mug. "Look, Bev. It's no secret. They *moved*. People move. You moved *here*, right?"

"I'm from here. I came back. The Spectres were from here, too. Where are they going?"

"Is this about teacher turnover?" Darry asked, dropping the empty packet and staring at Beverly full-on. "Or is it about something else?"

He was onto her. Of course he was onto her. Beverly flipped her notebook closed. "This is a good start, Darry. Next, I'd love to take a look at your employee handbook and records of in-house disciplinary action against any faculty members in the past five years."

"We can't share information on personnel. You *know* that's confidential, Bev." He leaned back, lacing his fingers behind his head and sighing.

"Not the handbook. That's board approved. As are any board meeting minutes."

"Not special meetings."

Beverly cocked her head. "You know, you're right, Darry."

"About?" He lifted one eyebrow, seemingly just half interested.

"This story isn't about teacher turnover at all."

That got his attention. "Then what is it about?"

She stood, tucking her notebook into her bag and pulling out a ten-dollar bill. She slid it under her untouched mug and set her jaw at Darry. "This story is about something much more concerning."

CHAPTER 4—QUINN

After everything was ready for the luncheon, Quinn went home to change into something nice.

She returned within half an hour, wearing a bright red blouse tucked loosely into the front of a pair of high-waisted white jeans. They were classic bell bottoms, and she'd found them at the Penny House, a thrift store in town. But high-waisted bell bottoms were back in style, and Quinn figured they were flattering, too.

Plus, if any of the other moms knew about her recent history as a delinquent mother (more or less), she'd have to fight against that. So, stylish and neat might sell her to them a little better than homely and unkempt.

Annette's house had come alive in those thirty minutes. Only two unfamiliar cars abutted the sidewalk on Apple Hill Lane, but inside, there were seven new faces. This, Quinn had come to learn, was classic Harbor Hills. Carpools and footpaths took precedence over convenience and status. A contradiction, in some ways, since most of the people Quinn had met were nothing short of perfect.

"You must be *Quinn*," a forty-something redhead chirped, already halfway through her mimosa. "Quinn Whittle? Love that name," she added, her eyes wide.

Quinn shrugged. "Thanks, I guess." She remembered her manners. "And you are...?"

"Jody Gladstone." She shot her hand out and, when Quinn took it, pumped enthusiastically. "We live up the way on Pine Tree Place. My husband's on the board."

Quinn desperately wanted to ask which board. Seemed like there might be a lot of those around Harbor Hills. Instead, she nodded like she knew and smiled as naturally as she could muster. "Right, yes."

"Your husband commutes?" Jody asked, but something in her tone and her expression told Quinn this woman already knew all about Matt Fiorillo and Quinn's past.

Quinn gave brief consideration to lying. She blinked and licked her lips. "Divorced."

"Oh!" Jody's eyes lit up, and she twisted her head to the rest of the party. "Miriam!" she called out before returning her attention to Quinn. "Miriam Cranefeld is divorced, too!" She looked wildly about the room. "Where is she?"

Again, Quinn flushed. In her world, divorce wasn't a point of pride or a special commonality to share with other women. At least, it hadn't been until now.

Thankfully, though, Jody left to track down the other token divorcée of the Hills District PTSO.

Meanwhile, Quinn found Annette in the kitchen, frantically refilling champagne glasses. "This is a thirsty bunch!" Annette declared.

"I'll help." Quinn would much rather be the help than a guest, in fact. But it soon became clear that all those present had the same mindset. Soon enough, the group of nine had all squashed into the kitchen, fussing over the spread of appetizers and offering help—*demanding* to help Annette somehow.

At last, once each woman had a full plate and refilled glass, they congregated in Annette's living room, an unwelcoming space that Quinn had learned was mainly for show, rather than comfort.

"Okay, ladies," Annette sang out, effectively earning herself the attention of everyone in the room.

Quinn leaned forward to peer through the windows at the backyard. Sure enough, Vivi and Elijah stood at adjacent sides of the slipshod wooden structure, each with hands on hips, studying it in comic seriousness. Quinn longed to be out there, to rake her fingers through her daughter's hair and whisper, *Don't do it. Don't grow up.*

"Quinn?"

She snapped from her reverie and leaned back into the stiff white fabric of the love seat, her back meeting with a never-broken-in throw pillow. Comfort could be just weeks away, Quinn thought, if Annette would only let it in.

Looking toward the voice that had called to her, her eyes landed on her friend. "Sorry?" she asked, by way of a request to repeat the question.

"Anything you want to add to our mission statement?"

Quinn knitted her brows together and studied the printout in her hands. "Oh, right." She glanced back over it. "The mission of the Hills Parent-Teacher-Student Organization is to unite all stakeholders in support of the public education of Harbor

Hills students in a loving, positive, and productive provision."

"It's lovely," she confirmed, nodding and pressing her lips together in a smile. "Really nice."

"I have one little thing to suggest," a dark-haired woman interjected. "The word *loving*. Does it...*suggest* something?"

Her inquiry was met with a roll of sighs, and Quinn found a weak spot in this would-be tightknit group. *Word choice.*

Soon, though, she found she'd gotten it wrong. It wasn't the word choice. Something else. Darker.

"This is about Christie Spectre, isn't it?" Jody accused. Suddenly, her red hair turned dull. Her bright eyes narrow and shadowed.

"We're not going there!" Annette cried, hands slicing the air in determination. The room fell silent, and Annette smiled. "Now, then. Do I have a motion to reword the mission?"

No one answered.

Annette pressed on. "That settles it. Next up!" she referred to her own printout, and Quinn studied her. Annette wasn't ordinarily cranky or short with others. At least, not in Quinn's purview. So why was she acting that way now?

A different woman chimed in. "Budget over-view," she offered meekly.

Off they took, discussing funds and spending and all the most boring details in the world. Quinn felt herself zoning out just as the agenda took another turn. "Now," said Annette, cool as ice, "the most important matter of business."

Silence overtook the room again, but this one was different. *Deferent.*

Quinn steeled herself.

Annette stood up for this agenda item, sweeping the bottom of her dress and smoothing its front. "We need to address the elephant in the room."

CHAPTER 5—JUDE

It was Monday, the second-to-last Monday of August, and in just one week, Jude would be due to report for new-teacher orientation. Before then, she hoped to suck the last drops of summer from Harbor Hills. This meant, for Jude, a few girlfriend dates.

In fact, she had three lined up for the week ahead: that afternoon she'd lunch with Quinn, on Wednesday, a walk around the block with Annette, and on Saturday, Jude was having Beverly over to help her decide on some budget-friendly renovations. Beverly had such a nice, classy home, and Jude could see the woman needed something *more*. Something to do with her extra time. Something to look forward to. To distract her.

Noon rolled around, and Jude arrived at Eat Street, parking in the narrow gravel lot to the side of the building.

Jude made her way into the kitschy café and asked for a table for two.

Sitting with her menu and a plastic tumbler of water, she tucked a strand of hair behind her ear and kept an eye out for Quinn. The previous week, she'd gotten a new cut and color and felt a little more like her old self, at least in regard to personal maintenance. Her new hair color, though, was a change. She'd opted for the silver look, rather than keeping up with the buttery blonde she'd been striving for since, well, since she'd actually *been* blonde.

Red lipstick paired well with the silver locks. And since she didn't want to put out the cash for a manicure, Jude did her own nails at home. A clean beige polish over squared-off, trimmed nails. Classy. That was the goal as summer fell to autumn. *Class*. It was how Jude would get through the switch in seasons.

See, that was Jude's Achilles' heel. Change. She had an aversion to it. It was the hardest thing about marriage to Gene, too. Except for, well, the obvious other hard thing. Gene was a mover and a shaker. He lived for weekend getaways and spur-of-the-moment trips.

But Jude had never much appreciated surprise.

She was learning to, though.

The chime above the door rang and a *whoosh* pulled the air conditioning out with it. In stepped a tall, stylish blonde. Quinn.

Jude held up a hand, and she saw it right away, smiling and slipping into the corner booth at the back.

"So glad you could make it," Jude said. "I forgot that you work now."

Quinn waved her off and unfolded the menu. "Only here and there. My job with the paper is mostly work-from-home. Plus, I can do a lot of it in advance. Scheduling posts, all that."

Jude was fascinated with Quinn's job. To her, it felt a little silly. Making Facebook posts and curating an Instagram account. Still, Jude reserved her opinions for herself, preferring friendship over judgment. Perhaps for the first time in her life. Sad.

"It sounds like fun," Jude managed.

"Hm?" Quinn glanced up from the menu, refolded it. "Oh, my job. Right." She seemed contemplative about it, and after a moment gave a short, sure nod. "I like it. It's different."

"What is your dream job?" Jude propped her chin in her hands, her elbows on the table. It had been a long time since she'd had a one-on-one like this. She felt inspired.

Quinn, for her part, looked surprised. "Oh! My dream job." Frowning, she thought again for a while, as if hazy and distracted. "I'm not sure I have one, to be honest."

Jude reared back. "Huh." This response caught her off guard, for some reason. "As a little girl? You didn't want to be a veterinarian or a ballerina?"

"I played house a lot," Quinn answered, the dreamy quality returning and her face softening in reflection. "I was always the mom. Or about to be. I liked to stuff a blown-up balloon under my shirt and waddle around my house."

Immediately, Jude conjured an image. "Are your parents still alive?"

Quinn's eyes flashed. "Yes and no."

The waitress plopped down two mugs of coffee. "What'kin I getcha girls?" she asked, her Midwestern accent in full effect.

Synchronously, Jude and Quinn each said her order. Quinn flushed and held her hand up. "You go."

"Sally's Famous Sweet Roll," Jude said with all

the awkwardness of a woman who normally opted for an egg white omelet.

"Mm," Quinn hummed. "Make it two." She smiled at the waitress and passed up her menu. Jude followed suit, never taking her eyes from Quinn.

"You look happy."

Quinn blinked, her head jerking back. Then, a smile broke out along her lips. "Thanks," she answered, a knit in one eyebrow. "I think I am."

Jude nodded. "It's a good feeling, happiness." She brushed a strand of her silvery hair from her eyes and took a long sip of her drink. "Is it the job? Vivi?"

"Vivi, of course. Having her back is all I wanted." Quinn stopped, suddenly distracted by her own thoughts. "Actually, that's what I always wanted to be. A mom."

"Then that'll do it all right."

"It's more than that, though." Quinn paused, her gaze settling on Jude fixedly.

Jude cocked her head, listening.

"It's you and Annette. Beverly, too. Having friends around."

"That's new for me, actually," Jude confessed.

"New? Haven't you lived on Apple Hill for a while?"

"Oh, yes. A long time. But I've had a rough decade or two." Jude chuckled mirthlessly. "Or three or four or five—"

"Come on," Quinn interrupted. "You're telling me you've had less than a life of charm and perfection? *You?* Jude Banks?"

"I wasn't always Jude Banks," Jude answered cryptically. She waved it off. "Anyway, what I mean is that it's been a good month or so, with you moving in. You've brought us together in a way that a common road never could."

"I don't know if it was me who did that," Quinn replied. "I'd rather think it was my house."

A snorting chortle erupted from Jude's mouth. "No." She shook her head.

Quinn smirked. "What?"

Again, Jude shook her head. "Take it from me. Houses don't fix things."

CHAPTER 6—BEVERLY

Darry wouldn't talk. Sources with their lips zipped was one of the more aggravating aspects of reporting. For some journalists, a challenge like this lit a fire. It motivated them. Not Beverly. Her angle was almost always softer. Gentler. Never provocative or aggressive. Quiet and careful.

But there was one thing that bothered her more about her job than tough leads, and that was a boring story to begin with.

The tale of Hills High teacher turnover was so *mundane*, Beverly decided between that and Darry's choice to remain mum, she'd move on. The Monday following her dead-end interview at Eat Street, she told her boss she would set her sights once again on the Carl Carlson case.

Now, Beverly set about digging in.

She began with the Harbor Hills Public Library.

A narrow two-story erected in the forties, the library suffered from a bad case of clinging to the past. Either that, or abysmal funding. Knowing Harbor Hills, it could be either, or, more likely, *both*. Normally, Beverly could appreciate nostalgia. But now, it meant that she'd have to comb through annals of microfilms. This task, while quaint, was far more time-consuming than a simple internet archives search.

Even so, she settled in for an afternoon of slides, thumbing perfunctorily through the best she could think of: dated editions of the *Herald*.

Beverly had plans to meet with her neighbors later in the week, and she'd curated a list of questions for each of them, too. First, though, it would be useful to have the basics down.

After two hours of scanning, she'd come up with exactly nil. In the time range she'd narrowed—the early nineties—there had been no fuss made over 696 Apple Hill Lane nor its penultimate resident. Carl Carlson, it would seem, lived a very quiet life on Beverly's street.

Maybe even *too* quiet.

Just as she was about to call it a day and pack up, an obituary, of all things, caught her eye.

Beverly stopped the wheel and read the words once. Twice.

CARL CARLSON,

Former resident of Detroit Carl Bernard Carlson died Dec. 23, 2005, at his home in Harbor Hills, Mich. Due to the circumstances surrounding Mr. Carlson's death, no service will be held. Carl was assumed to hail from the local Carlson clan, a prominent family of early Harbor Hills settlers known for developing the land and establishing the community's first and persisting sanitation and waste endeavor. Mr. Carlson leaves no known local kin, although it is likely he has a female descendant still living. In lieu of flowers, the town respectfully requests that donations are made to Harbor Hills Historical Society.

BEVERLY TAPPED a finger to her bottom lip. It was an odd obituary. Unusual. There had to be more to the story, but how could she find it?

It had been ages since Beverly had covered

something *real*. Something deep and dark. Who did she go to back then? When she wrote the piece about the town manager embezzling tens of thousands of taxpayer dollars...or when she tried to track down leads on the case of the missing Detroit woman. What was her name? Beverly couldn't quite recall. Something with a *T*. Something odd.

Anyway, with every single substantial news story, Beverly had a single, useful source.

Her very own mother.

CHAPTER 7—QUINN

I t turned out that the women of Harbor Hills had low standards for awkward. During the PTSO luncheon, they made a huge fuss over the fact that there was a distinct dearth of diversity on the PTSO. And not the sort of diversity a city-wise gal like Quinn would think of.

Diversity in the P *and the* T *and the* S, *you see,* Annette had interpreted for Quinn. *We can't only have parents on the PTSO! We need teachers and students, too!*

The elephant in the room.

After a long, boring back-and-forth between Jody-the-Redhead and the woman called Miriam, they agreed that it was best to reach out to a specific teacher, rather than make an all-call.

Anyway, even if there was such a thing as open season in the PTSO, Quinn suspected teachers would shrink away from the chance, rather than run to it.

By meeting's end, they came to the agreement to pitch the idea to a special teacher *after* school began. This gave the ladies of PTSO a chance to eye an educator who'd make a difference.

In the interim, the PTSO had other matters. Back-to-school brunch for the faculty, the Fall Festival for the elementary, and helping to advertise the winter production of *The Sound of Music*, set to play in early December.

But Quinn had more in her life to worry about than just those to-dos of her new club. She had her job to think of. And then, of course, she had her own back-to-school business. Namely, with Vivi.

Tuesday, Annette said she was free, and they could take the kids shopping.

Quinn was equal parts excited and nervous for this double date, of sorts. She hadn't found much shopping in downtown Harbor Hills, apart from the Penny House. And she had little interest in driving to Birch Harbor for shopping, but even that locale lacked any retailers that would offer both ladies' and young men's fashion.

A knock came at the front door at quarter after ten. Vivi answered, bouncing downstairs and tearing the door open. Quinn left the kitchen to join her daughter and, presumably, Annette.

It wasn't Annette, though. Just Elijah.

Vivi had already passed through the door, and they were halfway down the porch stairs by the time Quinn got there, her eyes searching the curb for Annette's car.

"Where's your mom?" she called after Elijah, confused.

He stopped and turned on the bottom step, sheepish. "Oh, hi, Ms. Whittle. My mom said she called you?" he answered as a question.

Quinn felt her body as if her cell phone was somewhere attached. It wasn't, of course. "About shopping?"

Vivi rolled her eyes. "My mom never has her phone." Then, she tugged her own phone free from her back pocket and flashed it toward Quinn. "Emergency HOA meeting. Elijah and I are going next door to work on the fort again."

The two teenagers dashed off, cutting across the lawn and back toward the Bests' side yard gate.

This was parenting a teenager. Things changed on a dime. Impulses drove the days. But God forbid

Quinn change the plans. Vivi would run away all over again, no doubt. She folded her arms and watched as the two disappeared behind the white pickets and the house beyond.

Then, mentally, she flipped to Vivi's response. Emergency HOA meeting. *What?*

As if on cue, Annette appeared on her porch, waving wildly at Quinn. "We're over here!"

Quinn let herself into Annette's house, following shushed, hurried voices to the kitchen.

There, huddled excitedly around the island, were Annette and Beverly.

"Elijah said there was an emergency with the HOA?" Quinn asked, bewildered.

Annette lifted a mischievous eyebrow. "I mean...*kind* of," she answered cryptically, leaning away from the island and pouring a glass of lemonade before offering it to Quinn. "Take a seat." Then, she raised a hand to Beverly. "She can explain."

CHAPTER 8—ANNETTE

Normally, Annette would cancel anything to go shopping. Especially on a beautiful, warm day when Roman was handling clients and her son was *actually* okay with being seen in public with his mother.

But when Beverly showed up that morning, alert and fresh and brimming with energy, Annette knew what she had to do.

The three of them settled at the kitchen table with a bowl of popcorn—appropriate—and their drinks. The curtains drawn, the women had a clear view of the kids. Something to ground them, as Annette said.

"Start at the beginning, Bev," she commanded, beaming at Quinn. Quinn, who was still confused about the canceled shopping trip. Quinn, who perhaps didn't appreciate small-town gossip quite yet. Quinn, who blinked quickly three times and twisted her lemonade in her hands, studying the rim as if to inspect how well Annette had cleaned it.

Quinn, who needed someone else's drama for once.

Beverly launched into her overview.

"The teacher turnover piece is dead in the water. Going nowhere." She glanced away as she said it. "I'm switching gears. I think I mentioned before that I was interested in pursuing the Carlson case?" At her question, Beverly met Annette's gaze then Quinn's.

"What case?" Quinn asked, frowning and turning to Annette. "I thought he was older."

Annette pursed her lips, leaned back, and folded her arms over her chest. "He was. Elderly, from what I know."

"Do you know anything else?" Beverly pinned Annette with a hard stare. She hadn't even gotten through her overview.

"I thought *you* were coming here to tell *us* what happened," Annette replied, amused by her neighbor's suddenly changed disposition. The prior despondence and melancholy had been replaced. Was it temporary? Annette wondered.

"I don't have much to tell. *Yet.*" Beverly mirrored Annette and crossed her arms. She blinked and leaned forward to look at her notepad before leaning back. "Basically, I think there's more to Carl Carlson than meets the eye." She relaxed and reached for her drink but didn't sip from it.

"So, what *do* you have to tell?" Quinn asked, grinning.

Annette nodded in agreement, thirsty for gossip.

Beverly sucked in a deep breath and looked around. "I know that Carl Carlson died in the home, obviously. I know that his obituary was weird. And I know that there was more to the Carlson family than we even realize."

"What do you mean? How do you know?" Quinn asked, rapt.

Beverly shrugged. "I called my mom. She's part of the old generation. The one that holds the town secrets."

"And?" Annette asked, wide-eyed.

"She's in Birch Harbor for the week."

Quinn's face fell. "Who is running the bed-and-breakfast?"

"She blocks it out for a week. Every year in

August she goes to the harbor to soak up the lake water like a fish and flounce around with her old-timey friends."

"But did she tell you anything?" Annette asked, eyeing Beverly hard.

"Not yet. She was *busy*." Beverly rolled her eyes like a teenager. "She'll be back home this weekend, and I made her promise we would do breakfast."

"I want to go!" Annette joked. Half joked, rather. She didn't even know what was supposed to be so fascinating with Carl Carlson and here she was, glomming on to Beverly and Beverly's mom, Bertie.

"You can come. We can make it a girls' brunch!"

"It's the Saturday before school starts," Quinn said. "What better way to celebrate?"

"True," Annette agreed. "We can celebrate and brunch." She smiled. After all, there was no greater female bonding than bonding over small-town lore. And if it was a Saturday, Jude could join.

"Saturday brunch it is," Beverly confirmed. "But before we get to that, the reason I came over was because I had questions." Beverly leveled her gaze squarely on Annette.

Annette giggled nervously. "Like, questions for Quinn and me? About Carl?"

Beverly nodded mock gravely. "Specifically,

about his house. Quinn's house, I guess. And maybe Apple Hill Lane more broadly."

The shape of Annette's lips pinched into a smirk and she winked at Quinn. "What do we know? We just *live* here."

CHAPTER 9—JUDE

Over the week, Jude made good progress in her classroom. She'd pulled down the previous teacher's old posters and cleaned out the desk, sorting everything small into a cardboard banker's box and propping everything not so small against the box by the door.

In the course of her cleanout, she'd pieced together some information about the woman whose place she'd be taking. A lady by the name of Mrs. Spectre. One of two Spectres at Hills High. It reminded Jude of her own relationship with Gene. How they met at a conference. He a principal, she early in her administrative training, eager to network, connect, and kiss up.

The Spectres, however, were on even playing field, it would seem.

At least, that was the rumor flitting around when Jude ducked into the teachers' lounge for a quick bite or to run off copies.

She was anxious to share the information with Beverly, knowing full well that Beverly was doing a story on teacher turnover. Maybe the Spectres were a big part of the story. It was early to tell, and early to intrude, but Jude wasn't sure where her priorities lay. With the school and her career? Or with Apple Hill Lane and her neighbor-friends?

Earlier on in the week—Tuesday afternoon— she'd gotten a text invitation to join her neighbors for a brunch at Bertie's B&B. At the time, she had worried she would be too busy.

Jude had told Annette she was a soft maybe. After some needling by the woman, Jude upgraded to a hard maybe.

But it wasn't until Friday that Jude *knew* she'd go.

It wasn't until Friday that she uncovered something so juicy, she'd be wrong not to join her new friends and divulge.

Standing in her classroom, the last Friday before the first day of school, Jude gripped the pink sheet. So thoughtlessly crammed in the depths of a drawer, stuck like a piece of white paper, crimped and crunched by the inner workings of a Xerox machine.

Proof. Of something.

Briefly, Jude contemplated taking a photo and texting it to Beverly. That would be crass, though. Unethical. Could even get her into trouble.

Instead, as she packed up her satchel—a leather thing with a floppy flap and worn strap—she smoothed the thin pink page and slipped it between her full-size daily planner and the teacher handbook she hadn't yet cracked open.

SATURDAY MORNING, Jude awoke and took an early cup of coffee on her back deck, alone. She noticed the very slightest nip in the air, like Harbor Hills was preparing for the fall of summer to autumn. Like the town knew Labor Day and the start of the school year would propel the world into a tidal wave-sized change. Mothers would rediscover their freedom. Teachers and students, their imprisonment.

Jude fell somewhere in the middle of the range of sovereignty. A teaching job would afford her more money, though not much more. And it'd afford her a place in Harbor Hills society she couldn't otherwise have gained. As one of the town servants. The town workers. On the other hand, gone would be her precious days of lounging or gardening or reading.

The nip in the air broke and warmth rushed the porch, now swathed in sunlight, its eastern exposure a source of irritation for Gene, once upon a time. He'd been more of a night-owl type, shunning early mornings and irritating rays cutting across the kitchen, exposing air heavy with dust.

Jude had liked it. Good light showed her what needed cleaning.

After washing her single mug and drying it, she ran a cloth over her counters and got ready for breakfast. It'd be her first time at Bertie's, even though she knew of the place.

It was ten to eight when she pulled up outside Bertie's, having preferred to drive herself despite offers of rides from each of her neighbors. She felt she needed the quiet time in her car. Both before *and* after the brunch.

Sitting a moment, Jude rolled her windows down to catch a little fresh air. Comfortable, if anxious, she reached for her purse and removed the folded pink page, opening it and smoothing it across the dash as if to prepare it for a presentation.

She hesitated, wondering if this was wrong. Her ethics and morals bubbled to the surface.

Jude licked her lips and reviewed the document with its faint notes and nearly imperceptible details.

No.

This *was* wrong. She began to refold the page when a voice startled her from just outside her car window.

"Oh, no."

CHAPTER 10—BEVERLY

Beverly frowned deeply and added, "Don't tell me that's a parking ticket." She cocked her head sympathetically to Jude, knowing that if there was anyone on the street who might offer up more info on Carl Carlson, it would be Jude.

Jude Banks—or Jude Carmichael—had lived on Apple Hill Lane the longest out of all of them. Even longer than Beverly, though Beverly was a local.

And while Beverly suspected Jude had deeper roots in the area, she still wasn't sure exactly *who* Jude was, where she came from, or what her story was.

Beverly, awash in new hope and new drive, figured that if she could learn about each of her neighbors, she might learn more about Carlson.

And if she could learn more about Carlson, then she could write a great piece. And if she could write a great piece, then...well, maybe she *would* have something to live for these days.

Jude popped her door open, but the pink page had disappeared. A wide smile painted Jude's face. "Hah! No. Just a—some paperwork from school." She pushed out of the car, closed the door, and locked it with her fob, testing the handle by way of a few quick tugs.

Beverly tucked a strand of hair behind her ear and walked alongside Jude. "Are we still on for our previous arrangement at your house?" she asked, finding herself suddenly and delightfully overbooked.

Beverly *needed* to be overbooked. Even her own boss and cousin, Forrest Jericho, had suggested she pursue both the teacher turnover feature *and* the Carl Carlson feature. "It'll keep you busy," he sang out as she left work on Friday.

Even so, if her hunch was right, the Carlson story had enough to fill her days until, at the very least, the first week of school was over and the hurt from the year before felt more doable.

"We're on!" Jude confirmed, shifting her bag up higher on her shoulder.

Beverly smiled back, and together they paused at the white gate in front of Bertie's. Jude stared it at with reverence. At least, that's how Beverly saw her.

"I can't believe this has been in your family for generations," Jude admired.

Beverly shrugged. "I don't think about it much, honestly."

"Did you grow up here?" Jude asked as Beverly pushed through the gate and led the way toward the house.

"No. Well, yes and no. We had a normal house on Griggs Street. That's where we *lived*. But yeah, I was here a lot." Beverly smiled at the memory. Sometimes, growing up, she'd help her mother at the inn, turning beds and cleaning the bathrooms. Work that Beverly didn't much mind. Sometimes, she'd steal away in the parlor with a book until Bertie was relieved of her shift by the night girl. "What about you?" she asked Jude, more out of politeness than curiosity.

But they were interrupted. "Welcome to Bertie's!" her mother declared from the open door. "You're Judith!"

Jude, who wasn't all that much younger than Bertie, now that Beverly thought about it, rose to the occasion. That's how it was with Beverly's mom.

People either shrank away from her or met her where she was.

Interesting to see Jude find her voice. "Call me Jude," she replied, accepting a warm hug ahead of Beverly.

"Jude, right." Bertie gave Beverly a hug, too, and ushered them inside. They exchanged easy small talk and waited for the balance of the guests— Annette, Quinn, and Viviana—who showed up over the next fifteen minutes.

Beverly did not need to make further introductions, as Bertie had already been acquainted with the other ladies. So instead, she coordinated seating arrangements around the dining room table—a long and broad Edwardian piece that her early ancestors had lugged in right after they'd built the house, a narrow and towering Victorian that hid behind a thatch of maples at the back end of Main Street.

Mimosas were poured—and an orange juice for Vivi—and plates were neatly filled, each with eggs Benedict, a pastry, and a small bowl of fresh fruit. The women made casual conversation as they dove into the splendid spread. Beverly felt proud of her mother and of the B&B. That pride coupled with the excitement of what she was about to do was enough of a distraction that having Vivi around didn't bother Beverly.

She shouldn't bother Beverly. Of course she shouldn't. But how could a beautiful young teenager full of life and potential and a future *not* bother Beverly?

"Beverly," Bertie purred, patting her red lips with a navy-blue cloth napkin. She cleared her throat and eyed Beverly, who knew what was coming. Her mother had already been primed and prodded. She knew exactly what Beverly needed to know, but if one thing could be counted on, it was that Bertie Gillespie would orchestrate the brunch like a finely organized presentation. Indeed, she said, "You've called us together. I can't stand the suspense. Tell us, other than for the camaraderie and good cheer, *why* are we here today?"

CHAPTER 11—QUINN

As Beverly launched into an overview of her story, Quinn shifted uncomfortably in her seat. The last time she was at the bed-and-breakfast, Vivi had run away. Being back there now, even under starkly different circumstances, Quinn didn't share Bertie's enthusiasm for the food and gossip. Okay, well, not the *gossip*.

Plus, Quinn, like everyone else, *knew* what Beverly had up her sleeve. She was now just playing along, as she had precious little to contribute.

Adjusting her remaining clean silverware—a spoon and a knife—into straight, parallel lines, Quinn blinked twice, holding back that third blink with all the force she could muster.

She tuned back in to Beverly's summary.

"It's a hunch. I have a hunch that something is fishy about Carl Carlson. And at the very least, the fact that *no* one in Harbor Hills knew him—that *alone* is a story."

"What do you mean?" Vivi asked boldly.

Annette pressed her lips together and cocked her head at Vivi. "Everyone knows everyone here." She raised a hand to Beverly. "She's accusing us of being *un*neighborly."

Beverly looked stricken. "No!" she shot back. It was the most energy Quinn had seen come from the woman...ever. This denial. "That's not true. And if you were unneighborly, then so was I. Anyway, I didn't mean that at all," she begged. "I meant that—" Beverly stopped and sucked her lips into her mouth. She looked worried and nervous, and her freshness waned.

"But Jude—" Quinn jumped in. "Jude went there, right? Jude's been in my house?"

"That's right!" Annette agreed, her previous accusation floating out of the dining room on a gust of new verve.

Jude appeared to turn defensive. "So?" she shot.

"So"—Vivi caught the momentum and ran with it—"that means you guys *tried*. You tried to befriend him or help him, right?"

"Right," Beverly agreed, her smile returning. "That's my point. It was never our fault that Carl was a ghost. And he wasn't your usual introvert. We never even met the guy, right?"

"Okay," Quinn said, "so, what is the angle for your story, Beverly?" As a colleague, she felt like she could help focus Beverly. Pin her to a working title or a slant.

Beverly took a breath and rolled her shoulders back. "Simple. Secrets of a Small-Town Recluse."

Quinn blinked. Again. A third time then scrunched her nose, irritated with her lack of self-control. Why was she anxious? She couldn't pin it down.

Until Jude spoke up. "Whoever said Carl Carlson had secrets?"

Next to Quinn, Vivi shifted in her chair. Her gaze turned icy but coy. "Who *doesn't* have secrets?"

CHAPTER 12—ANNETTE

Vivi was Annette's kind of gal. "She's right." Annette winked at the girl and gave a short nod. "And if everyone has secrets, then *everyone* has a story. It's just waiting to be told." Offering Beverly a firm stare, Annette knew that's what she needed. Not someone to undermine her work. Someone to fight with her. To fight for something—even if it wasn't some important truth about society or small-town scandal that needed to be aired out.

Sometimes, in order to get over your own past, you had to spend a little time in someone else's.

Even Annette knew as much. She went on. "Heck, Bev. You can write a story about me, if you want to."

"What story is there to tell?" Bertie roared into a round of laughter. "You're an open book, Annette Best!"

Annette couldn't help it. She laughed, too, at the joke. At herself. It was an armor she wore, actually. "You could write about how I'm losing my business and coordinating a house swap. How my marriage sucks because Roman thinks I want him to be something he's not."

White noise splashed over the table with the tinkering of forks against plates and ice cubes in glasses. Soon, the tide of the table noise rushed back out to sea, leaving everyone as cold and silent as a lonely buoy bell.

Annette swallowed, as shocked as anyone at what just fell out of her mouth. "I love Roman." It was all she could think to say.

Jude, who sat next to her, reached an arm around Annette's shoulders, pulling her into a side hug.

"Financial stress is the worst, they say," Quinn replied quietly.

Vivi flashed a fearful look at her mother. "Is that why you divorced Dad?"

Annette found her voice. "Let's not let this devolve. Beverly brought us here to talk about 696

Apple Hill Lane. Not *our* problems." She gave a sorrowful look at Bev. "Sorry. I just—"

"No. Don't apologize. We all have issues," Beverly answered.

"Heck if women don't carry the lot of them, either!" Bertie cried, her raspy voice crackling in the air.

"My point is simply that, Bertie. That none of us is free from a few skeletons. Some bigger than others," Annette said softly. She squeezed Jude's hand beneath the table in thanks. "Let's get back to Carl."

CHAPTER 13—JUDE

Jude felt itchy. Like she wanted to be anywhere else than an interrogation slash brunch. Sure, she was excited to make friends. But at what cost? Suffering the bored housewives' appetites for drama? Then again, of the five other women, only one was technically a wife at all anymore. And she wasn't a *house*wife. Annette had a career.

Jude held her tongue as Beverly pushed ahead with her theories.

"I happen to believe Carl Carlson did have secrets. He was an old, lonely man. Maybe they were boring ones. Like...he never married the love of his life or something. And he regretted that."

"Regrets make for the saddest secrets," Jude

murmured. It came from out of nowhere, the thought. She shouldn't have said it, either. Hurt clouded Beverly's eyes. Jude scrambled to smooth things out. "I just mean, not taking risks. People who play it safe. *That's* what I mean." And she did. She meant it about herself, too. Gene was not a risk. He was a safe bet, is what he was. Or at least, that's what he was *supposed* to be. The irony didn't escape Jude.

Beverly leveled her chin and went on. "Anyway, I think there's more to the story." Her eyes flashed at Quinn. "Have you finished cleaning? Is everything in the garage now, or—"

Quinn nodded. "Yes. We've cleared the house. I saved some of the bigger furniture pieces, but what we didn't sell at the yard sale is in the garage, for the most part. Anything with value, that is."

"Mind if I take a look later?"

"What's there to find?" Jude cut in, edgy still. She'd *really* hoped this would be more of a girls' day.

"Probably lots of stuff," Vivi answered on her mother's behalf. Then, to the whole table's surprise, the girl tugged free a pendant from the collar of her tank top. She held it up, the tarnished silver hardly glinting.

Jude stifled a gasp.

Annette did not. "You found that in 696?" she exclaimed, her hand pressed to her chest.

Quinn had a similar reaction. "What?"

Even Beverly appeared shocked, leaning in and squinting at the small medallion like it might have a secret message.

Vivi twisted it between her forefinger and thumb, holding it so Beverly could have the best view. "The plumber found it in the upstairs bathtub." She shrugged. "I thought it was cool in a creepy sort of way."

Jude chewed her lower lip. It was impossible to keep her curiosity over the necklace at bay. Like a charm from a bygone era, the discolored round drew her out. "What's it say there?" She fingered her own delicate chain then pointed to Vivi's neckline.

"It's a *B*," Vivi replied, frowning, her chin dipping into her chest as she strained to confirm. "At least I *think* so."

Quinn leaned over and pinched the top of the metal circle then squinted. "It looks like an eight."

Then Annette craned her neck to get a better look. "I don't think it's a letter *or* a shape. To me, it looks like a *symbol*."

"A symbol of what?" Beverly asked. Then, as if to cement her point, she added, "See? There's a story here." She looked at her mother as Jude took a long sip of coffee, savoring the last of its warmth as the liquid ran over her tongue and down her throat. The caffeine's effect was nearly immediate, like a punch to her heart and mind. A stroke of fresh energy. A mood booster.

Bertie cleared her throat. "It's a symbol, all right," she cracked. "A symbol of secrets. 'Carl Carlson' my *behind*," she huffed, her voice rising. "I never met anyone named Carl Carlson in my life! Not in Harbor Hills!"

Jude glanced Bertie's way then looked back to Beverly, who came alive at her mother's suggestion.

Beverly looked around the table, her expression wild. "*This* is why we're here." She stabbed a finger at her mother. "*She's* why we're here. Roberta Gillespie is Harbor Hills' own gossip columnist." Beverly leveled her chin and smirked. "She can tell us *everything*."

Jude smirked, too. "That is," she added, "if there's anything to be *told*."

CHAPTER 14—BEVERLY

Beverly shook her head at Jude. This was *so* Judith Carmichael. The crotchety sometimes-neighbor who quashed rumors and condemned idle blathering by the mailboxes.

Sighing, Beverly exchanged a quick and knowing look with Annette. In fact, Beverly herself wasn't much for talk, usually. She was more about writing it. In the paper. For money. That was the only time Beverly got caught up in local speculations. Gossip especially interested Beverly when the stories were verifiable and newsworthy.

Carl Carlson, she had a suspicion, was newsworthy. Even if *Jude* disagreed.

Beverly cleared her throat. "Listen, Jude," she said gently. "You haven't been around much, sure.

You're sort of"—she searched for a delicate way to approach the truth—"*new* here. Like Quinn." Beverly held a hand up as if to say, *See? You're not alone. Not everyone can be a* local.

Jude bristled and her eyes fluttered up in a half roll. But she crossed her arms and gave an indifferent shake of her head. "True," she murmured.

Beverly situated her recorder at the top right side of her plate, nearest her mother. Then, she flipped to a fresh page in her notebook. She flipped the whole book sideways and drew four vertical lines down. Columns. An extra wide one for Bertie, then equally sized ones each for Annette, Jude, and even Quinn. Her plan was to cross reference Bertie's memories against what the three others had heard, seen, or knew to be true— or *false*.

This was the second step in quality researching. The first had been hitting the library for basic info and brainstorming questions and leads.

"Mom?" Beverly set her jaw and gazed around the table. "We're ready."

Bertie's black eyebrows wriggled, and she pouted her red lips—still red after coffee and juice and breakfast—before dabbing her cloth napkin on them. Then, less gracefully, she poked her index finger into the blue fabric and swept it in the corners of her mouth, now an O.

She cleared her throat and ran her tongue over her teeth—top and bottom—then cleared her throat again. Finally, after sucking a deep breath into her heavily powdered nose, Bertie began.

"I don't know a *thing* about this 'Carl Carlson' character." She squinted one eye as she signed quotation marks in the air around his name. "And if you ask any old-timer here, they'll tell you the same thing. My bridge girls and me—we've talked him dead. The Ladies' Auxiliary, too. Not *once* did this man show up at church." Her eyes widened, and Beverly knew this was the group's cue to react.

She clicked her tongue for her mother's benefit. Annette shook her head. Quinn murmured "Hm" appropriately. Jude, to her credit, snorted. This clearly satisfied Bertie, who went on.

"I'm getting ahead of myself, though. Bev?" She looked thoughtfully at Beverly. "Do you remember when he first moved in?"

Beverly shook her head. "I was...in high school?"

"Ah, yes. The apathetic teenager phase." Her red lips pursed and twitched like she shared a secret with Beverly.

Beverly felt propelled to explain. "Carl moved in

in the midnineties or so, from what we know. When"—she sniffed and ran a finger beneath her nose—"Tom and I moved onto Apple Hill, he was already dead. Isn't that right, Mom?"

"Oh-five." Bertie nodded. "You came home that same year, Bev. Well, we only knew that anyone at all had moved into that house because the other properties came back to life, too."

"What do you mean?" Annette leaned in and frowned. "They had been around. My house. All five houses on Apple Hill were built decades earlier."

Bertie frowned, too. "It was all very confusing, you see. Your house, for example, Annette. It sold out of thin air."

"Yes, that's right. The Temper family bought it and rented it out. We were the first tenants. Roman convinced me we could buy just as soon as the business took off." Her chest filled and she leaned back, suddenly subdued.

"Temper family?" Beverly squinted. "I don't know a Temper family. Mom? Do you?"

"Temper? No." Bertie seemed miffed to be out of this particular loop.

"Property investors," Annette clarified. "At least, that's what I recall. I could be wrong."

"Do you remember Tempers moving in?" Beverly asked Jude.

Jude shook her head right away. "I never knew them. We bought our house around that time, but we weren't here. We mostly stayed around the island and Birch Harbor."

"Anyway," Bertie continued. "The only reason we knew, again, that someone had come in and taken up in that Apple Hill house was because signs went up. For Sale this and For Rent that. It was like the Carlson family finally decided to give up."

"Give up?" Beverly asked, scribbling everything down in shorthand. "What do you mean?"

"The Carlsons owned that whole neighborhood. Crabtree Court. It wasn't Crabtree Court until the HOA formed around the time you gals moved in. Before that, though, this old family had grand plans to do *something* with all that land. I mean, wouldn't you?" She didn't wait for an answer. "This old family with whom *my* family really collided. I recall Mother and Father continually having run-ins with Bernard and Irma. Like they just couldn't get along no matter what. Not with others around town and certainly not with each other."

CHAPTER 15—QUINN

"Bernard and Irma," Quinn murmured. "Those were the original owners of my house." It was taking her a bit to catch up, but she knew those names. They were *everywhere* in 696. In the paperwork and in dusty, warped photo albums. "But he went by Bernie"—she said it as more of a question—"I think?"

"Bernie, yes," Bertie confirmed, laughing. "That was the funny thing—Mother *hated* for me to go by Bertie, and Father said she only hated it because of *Bernie Carlson*. Bernie and Irma. Just insufferable people. They moved away years and years ago. To Detroit, I heard. One or the both of them was sick." She huffed, but her expression softened.

Quinn was lost. "Why? Sick with what?"

Bertie replied, "I think it was cancer. I regret to admit this, but no one much cared. Like I said, they weren't well loved here. Of course, Irma was worse by a mile. But ol' Bernie's association alone cost him local favor. Anyway, whoever it was who got sick, well, it happened after they lost Jeanette."

"Their daughter?" Beverly was writing in strange, looping symbols that reminded Quinn of her senior literature teacher in high school who sometimes taught secretarial notetaking.

Quinn nodded as she recalled that name, too. Less common in the home, but still present. Some photos had emerged of a young girl who appeared to turn into a teenager over the years. But, again, the photos were in such poor condition, it was hard to peg down much information about the girl. Sure, a child's bedroom had been left behind, buried beneath mounds of plastic-bagged clothing with plastic hangers poking through the tops. A pink quilt on a sturdy iron-frame bed. Matching white dressers, their edges worn in a way that was only now suggestive of a shabby-chic style, though clearly that wasn't the original intent. Time and hoarding had worn the furniture raw. Not an intent furniture designer.

Bertie confirmed Beverly's remark. "Jeanette

Carlson. Died in a car crash out of town. Of course, Jeanette had married off by then. Even had a child of her own. I don't know who she married or who the baby was. Anyway, Jeanette was Bernie and Irma Carlson's one and only child."

Jude mumbled, "Lots of us here."

Quinn cleared her throat. "Just like you, Viv." She elbowed her daughter playfully, but Vivi grunted.

"I'm not an only child, though."

Setting her jaw, Quinn contemplated ignoring the comment. Vivi was right. Technically, she did have a half sister in the world. Matt's doing, not Quinn's. But were the two really like sisters? No. Had they even known about each other before last year? Also, no.

Beverly turned the focus on Jude. "You don't have siblings?"

Jude flushed under the attention. She shook her head and picked up her glass of juice, downing it fervently.

Quinn watched as Beverly turned to Annette. "And you're an only child, too, aren't you?"

Annette shook her head. "Sister on Drummond Island. She never did have an interest in leaving home."

Quinn could tell she was up next for this odd, sidebar inquiry. "I have a brother."

"And I'm an only," Beverly noted lastly.

Bertie chuckled vulgarly. "It wasn't for lack of effort."

"*Mother*," Beverly hissed, and conversation returned to Bernie and Irma.

"Do *you* know anything about these two?" Annette asked Quinn, pinning her elbows to the table and folding her hands beneath her chin. "Bernie and Irma?"

Quinn blinked. "Oh. Um...not a lot. I've just seen some paperwork..." Her voice trailed off.

"What kind of paperwork?" Beverly dug.

Shrugging, Quinn stole a glance at Vivi. "I mean, you know. Bank statements. Tax returns. Some photos, too."

"Photos?" Bertie cut in, staring hard at Quinn. "So, you've probably seen pictures of that woman."

CHAPTER 16—ANNETTE

Annette hadn't the faintest idea of Bertie's reference. "What woman?" she asked, her mouth gaping and breath shallow with excitement. Small-town gossip was basically Annette's part-time job. She relished knowing *everything* there was to know about Harbor Hills.

Beverly, too, leaned in closer.

But Bertie shook her head. "There was a woman. Very strange. Years back. We weren't given much info, but—"

"But what?" Annette pressed, wide-eyed.

"In the nineties, like Bev said, the supposed Carlson brother moved in. Or whoever he was. No one ever got that much info, and the guy was totally quiet. At first, we were positive it was Bernie himself who moved in. However"—Bertie's eyes narrowed salaciously—"a girlfriend of mine did some snooping. Carl Carlson was the name. That's how we figured it might not be Bernie."

Quinn jumped in. "Some of the mail we found was addressed to Carl Carlson." She knitted her fingers together, tapping them against each other compulsively. "But still more of the mail left here was addressed to Bernard and Irma." She tapped her fingers faster and her eyes went with them, blinking.

Annette grinned to herself. Quinn's little quirks had endeared her to the women, and especially to Annette. In some ways, Quinn reminded her of Elijah, who also had a few mannerisms. As a child, he'd flapped his arms. Over time, this particular habit gave way to eye twitching, which then gave way to fiddling obsessively with his socks, which had *now* given way to a compulsive checking of his wallet. All of these behaviors flew under strangers' notice, to be sure. Not Annette's, though. And it was only when she stopped and reflected on her son that she gave the little ticks any mind. In truth, those Elijahisms were some of the things Annette loved best about her son. That made him who he was.

"Right." Bertie gave a sharp nod. "Carl Carlson

was the name. Anyway, he moved in, apparently, but that was all we ever knew. Until…"

"Until?" Beverly and Annette said it at the same time, both rapt.

"Until a woman appeared years later. Sporadically. Like, on holidays or over long weekends."

"Was it Jeanette?" Annette asked. "Was the woman Jeanette?"

"No." Bertie shook her head. "Remember, Jeanette had passed away by then. Anyway, this woman was younger than Jeanette would have been were she alive. We only knew there was a new woman at all because by then, Shamaine had purchased the house across the street."

"Shamaine was here then?" Jude asked blankly, finally partaking in the conversation after a period of silence.

"Oh, sure. Shamaine was born in town. Her husband founded Crabtree Court, you know."

"But how did he buy on Apple Hill? What exactly happened with the release of Apple Hill properties from the Carlsons to the general public? This was all private land, right?" Annette asked. She knew more real estate history than the average Joe, but that still wasn't much. The folded secrets of

Harbor Hills never did cease to amaze her, Annette, the nosiest of the neighbors.

Jude answered. "Bernie Carlson started selling the houses and land around the time"—she cleared her throat—"around the time he left for Detroit. If I'm not mistaken."

"Something like that," Beverly answered, scribbling again on her pad. She stopped and then looked up. "Wait, though. Jude, didn't you own first here? Or was it Gene who'd purchased your house?"

Jude scoffed. "I don't know if Gene and I were here before Shamaine or not. I mean...we were *never* around to encounter any neighbors. I didn't meet Shamaine until we'd been here a couple of years. Even then, I didn't dig around in her past." Annette detected a twinge of defensiveness in Jude but quickly chalked it up to her embarrassment about chasing Gene around Michigan during their marriage. Annette would never *chase* Roman like that. She'd be embarrassed to confess such a thing, too.

"Okay, well, regardless," Beverly pushed ahead, "let me just review my timeline."

And she did, starting with details about the Carlson family history—dating back to the turn of the century. Then the land development, that lane of colonials. She added the marriage of Bernard to Irma, a girl from Birch Harbor. She covered Irma's death. Bernard's death. Carl Carlson's arrival. Carl's death. Carl's body found in the house among his hoard. Quinn's arrival. She stopped.

"If that's all you're doing," Bertie remarked, "putting together a biography of this man and a history of his house... Honey, I don't see you getting many readers."

"Then I'm not being clear on the mystery," Beverly retorted.

Annette, growing bored—or confused, perhaps —folded her arms over her chest and leaned away from the table. "I agree with Bertie," she said. "But there *is* intrigue. I just can't pin it down."

Beverly replied with a churlish expression as she set her pen down and laced her fingers atop the notepad. "The intrigue stems from the fact that Carl Carlson didn't live in 696 alone."

CHAPTER 17—BEVERLY

The bombshell landed with a booming effect. The women twittered about who else could have been living in the house with Carl Carlson, and Bertie agreed that there had been *someone*. A woman or a man or *someone* other than that wisp of a young woman who was once or twice spied. All very odd, they agreed, but also all very much a dead end. Beverly had only come upon the point from a hunch, and little more.

So, conceding to the fact that even her own gossip-monger mother was useless, Beverly allowed the brunch to devolve into even more idle chatter.

Later that morning, Beverly was set to join Jude at Jude's house. Originally, when Beverly had agreed to help assess her home design needs, Beverly had accepted that Jude had invited her over as a charitable act. As a gesture of sympathy for the poor widow who was struggling to reemerge from her shell of grief.

But all during breakfast, Beverly couldn't help but notice it was Jude who seemed distracted. Quiet. Wrapped up.

This is why she didn't cancel and instead opted against dawdling to gossip with her mother. She left after a hug and a promise that she owed her mom a dishwashing. Then, Beverly left the B&B and met Vivi, Quinn, Annette, and Jude down the walk. Annette was wrapping up a quick phone call to check in on Elijah.

Both teens—Eli and Vivi—were heading to Annette's to continue their work on the backyard project Annette had set them to: tearing down the fort and hauling away the old lumber for scrap outside of town. Annette agreed to pay them with a night of pizza, pop, and cupcakes if they could finish before school started. Or so Annette had said. Beverly was trying hard to stop tuning out any mention of teenagers.

Once the call was over, Jude started by way of a warning, her eyes narrowed on Beverly. "Before we leave for my place, I have to caution you both: I'm on a tight budget."

Beverly shrugged. "Who isn't?" She wagged a finger at Jude. "You'd be surprised what you can do with a hundred bucks. If you're thrifty."

"But can I tear down wood paneling and repaint the interior for a hundred?"

The group stopped at the little white wooden gate in front of Bertie's. "Are you doing a demo?" Annette asked, ever nosy.

"Small renovations. That's all. Updates, really." Jude tucked a strand of her silvery hair behind one ear.

Annette snapped her fingers and hooked a thumb at Quinn. "Have you talked to Quinn?"

Jude shook her head.

Beverly realized where Annette was going. "Oh, yeah. Dean!"

Quinn chimed in, too. "You mean for a reno project?"

"Dean?" Jude continued to act befuddled, but Beverly and Annette exchanged a knowing look.

Quinn tried to help. "The Jericho guy?"

Beverly simply pursed her lips. "All those boys are handymen. I'll talk to Forrest at the office. We can get you a friends and family discount, I'm sure."

"Who are you friends or family of?" Jude asked now, almost suspicious.

"Dean, of course," Beverly answered. "I mean, he *is* my cousin. And his brother is my boss. Quinn's too. *And* I once went on a date with Dean's best friend." She grinned at the memory, feeling like her old self. Airy and free. She swallowed down the smile, Hills High and its infamous nooks and crannies coming into her brain like zombies.

But the smile fell away fast, because with the image of the high school came images of Kayla. Nausea took the place of fleeting joy, and Beverly's stomach roiled.

Jude cleared her throat. "You mean Dean, the electrician? Who helped Quinn?" She stammered, "I-isn't he...well...an *electrician*?"

"In a small town, *electrician* is just a pretense. Dean can do it all." Annette winked at Jude. "He's your man."

Now standing in Jude's foyer, Beverly peered around. Architecturally, it was much like her own. Beyond the white front door and well into the generous foyer was the staircase. White like the door and broad enough for two to pass one another. To the right of the foyer sat a narrow parlor with beige carpet that crawled up one step and into what likely was a dining room, although the carpet threw Beverly off.

"Amazing how our houses are all so similar looking."

"Mirror images of each other, I think," Jude commented.

"Quinn's has a more crowded effect, though. Like everything is closing in, I hate to say," Beverly remarked. "But it adds a coziness."

"Yes, well, hers is older, of course. Bernie's parents built that house before the turn of the century, I think."

Beverly twisted slowly the other way, noting how the living room gave way to the kitchen in a pseudo open concept. High above, white-painted wood beams carried east-west across the ceiling.

Everything was white or beige or cream. Reminiscent of Quinn's overall aesthetic, Beverly figured. But Quinn's home design had taken on color, as had her wardrobe, lately. Whites turned to reds and blues, greens, too. Now, in late August, Beverly couldn't help but wonder if Quinn's never-ending assortment of frost-colored jeans would disappear altogether.

Beverly scooped a finger into the neckline of her own blue blouse, tugging to pull air down along her skin. Jude's décor was nearly as stuffy as the temperature of her home, and Beverly found herself wondering how long she'd last without succumbing to her discomfort.

"So." Beverly clapped her hands together, shaking thoughts about architecture and temperature. "You said something about the paneling and paint? And this little half wall?" Beverly rested her hand on top of the painted wood. Also white. On the inside of it, nearest the women, was a glossy black bench beneath which stood a pair of galoshes and a little silver pail. Inside the pail, a shovel, pruning shears, and gardening gloves.

Beverly couldn't help but appreciate the perfect precision. Everything in its place. Everything exact. Calculated. Measured. Matching and flawless.

Flawless but *dated*. At least to Beverly's eye.

"Right." Jude strode to one wall and pressed her hand to it. "I painted all this a couple of years ago when white made a comeback. Before then, it was gray. I try to keep up with trends, but the paneling itself is now giving me nausea."

"Somebody made updates in the seventies, probably," Beverly reasoned.

Jude shook her head. "I think the paneling was here from the get-go. A cheap way to add character, maybe?"

Unfamiliar with decorative eras, Beverly simply shrugged. "Do you know if there's drywall behind? Is it true paneling or is this, I don't know, structural?" She knocked on the pony wall. A hollow thump came in reply. She knocked on the wall adjacent. It sounded much the same. "I mean, white is still *in*. And there is a sort of...character about the paneling, right?"

Jude pursed her lips. "I just want *different*, mainly. I mean, if I'm staying here, I can't look at the same walls I looked at when I was married to Gene."

Beverly swallowed and nodded slowly. "I understand."

A stricken expression cracked across Jude's features. "Sorry, Beverly. I know you—"

"I *understand*."

And boy howdy, *did* she.

"You painted your door."

Beverly nodded again. This was ground they'd already covered. A choice Jude had already complimented and Beverly had already explained away.

"Tom hated blue. Who hates the color blue, anyway? Who hates *any* color?"

Brittle laughter erupted from Jude. "I hate red and green. *Together*, I mean."

"Christmas colors," Beverly pointed out.

Shrugging, Jude sighed heavily. "Christmas is a sad time for me. Has been forever, I suppose."

"You hate Christmas?" Beverly found herself well and truly shocked. Who hated Christmas?

"No. I just—it doesn't carry much happiness." Then she glanced at Beverly and caved a bit. "Well, don't get me wrong. I'm as Catholic as they come. And Jesus's birth—I mean just don't get me wrong. But the celebration. The Christmas trees and gift exchanges and plum pudding." A crinkle formed between her eyebrows. "It's not my thing. I'm more of an Advent person. Midnight mass."

"So, you don't care for the colors because they represent something that makes you sad." Beverly stated it, rather than asked it. "People think I like blue because I have the blues. But blue is just my favorite color." She blinked, contemplating whether or not to say the next thing on her mind. The main thing on her mind. Would she sob? Would she faint? She said it anyway. "Blue was Kayla's favorite color, too." Surprised that she *didn't* sob or faint, Beverly tested one more admission, locking eyes with Jude. "And he still hated it." Mirthlessness filled her voice and the threat of tears dried up and tumbled down the back of her throat.

Jude shifted her weight and tucked her purse into the wicker basket that spanned two of her stairs. Longaberger, probably. Then, she walked into the parlor and sat in one of two matching crème-colored wingback chairs. Without an invitation to do the same, Beverly lowered into the other chair, perching hesitantly on the edge.

"It's okay," Jude murmured.

Beverly frowned, unsure *what* was okay.

Jude explained. "It's okay if you hated him, too."

CHAPTER 18—JUDE

Renovations be darned. Their façade of a home improvement meeting had swiftly shifted into part two of girls' day out. Or girls' day *in*, as was now the case.

Jude saw that this was her chance to help Beverly.

And maybe herself, too. In a way.

Moments before, Beverly had been on the brink of tears. Now, she was on the brink of something else. Something totally separate from her blue front door or her blue blouse or blue bracelets or...

Or something totally connected.

"You had trouble. All marriages do," Jude reasoned softly as she returned to the parlor with two sherries, her therapeutic beverage of choice.

Beverly's face hardened then turned blank. "I loved him." She said it like it was a simple fact. Like one might say grass is green or water is wet.

"You told me he didn't want the door painted blue," Jude said. It wasn't meant as an argument. More as a memory.

"What man wants that? It's minor. It's less than a crack or a fissure in a marriage. The color of a door, right?"

And she was right. Jude knew Beverly was right, but she also knew that there was more to the story. Quite a bit more.

"What about Kayla, Beverly?" Jude said it low, almost inaudible.

"What about her?" Beverly turned defensive. "She didn't care about the color of the door," she shot back through a cackle. "Kayla was easy. And I thought of myself as easy, too." The tension broke a bit, and Jude accepted that prying would get her nowhere.

"You always seemed that way to me. The quietest neighbors we could have hoped for, I always told Gene." Even saying his name felt like a mountainous thing. Maybe she and Beverly had this in common. This *husband* issue.

Beverly must have heard something in her voice. "I can't picture you together," she said.

Jude hadn't expected to take a turn under Beverly's magnifying glass. She tucked a strand of her hair behind her ear, pulling it tight so it'd stay there for once, and then took a sip of her drink. "It's early for sherry," she acknowledged, by way of changing the subject. "My mother was terrible about that." She laughed at the warm memory. A memory that should *not* be warm.

Beverly reverted to her initial question. "Did Gene ever even *come* to Harbor Hills? I can't picture *him* at all, come to think of it. Seems like he wasn't here. *Ever*." She emphasized the *ever*. Judgey. Jude considered a defensive stance, but then—what was there to defend? Certainly not Gene.

"Tall. Prematurely white-haired. Beady eyes. Cocksure and cavalier." Jude took another sip, relishing the nutty dryness. Sherry bit like a punishment, and that's how Jude liked it. Why she liked it, actually.

"Sounds like a catch," Beverly joked. "Tom was always handsome. 'Til the bitter end."

Now, there was more to her words, Jude knew. She frowned. "What happened to your school story?

Turnover at the Teenagery?" A wry smile curled over her lips.

"Now that's a title. *Teenagery*," Beverly replied, smiling and taking her first sip of the drink then recoiling. "I thought sherry was supposed to be sweet."

"Sometimes it is." Jude lifted the drink to her lips. "Sometimes it isn't." She sipped, swallowed, and swirled the remaining tawny liquid in her crystal goblet. "You know you'll have a source in me, right?"

Beverly looked at her, surprised. "A source?" But darkness fell again over her features. "You mean if I cover the high school turnover thing." She shook her head. "I—can't. It's too soon."

Jude forced herself not to slump. Instead, she shook her hair off her shoulders and rolled her shoulders back. "So, you're chasing down this Carl Carlson story instead? You really think there's something there?"

"There has to be," Beverly confirmed.

"What if there's not?" Jude studied her over the rim of her crystal, the bottom of Beverly's face blurred by the stippled glass.

"Well"—Beverly raised an eyebrow and stared beyond Jude for a thoughtful moment—"then I suppose I'll have to go back to the *teenagery* and find out the truth."

Jude's glare turned on Beverly like fire. "The truth about what? The high school's turnover rates?"

Beverly gave one firm shake of her head, but the surface of the sherry shook in her trembling hands. "To find out the truth about my husband."

CHAPTER 19—BEVERLY

The start of school came and went, and Beverly spent the days inside her house, huddled in shelter against the world. A world that continued to turn in spite of her.

Forrest, her editor, had given her permission to work from home that particular week. In a surprising bout of selfless awareness, he'd called her Sunday and told her it was fine if she wished to lay low.

She did.

Still, she had work to do. After her sherry-induced chat with Jude, she'd agreed that the Carlson thing could be a dead end, and a dead end would help no one, least of all herself. Instead, she'd return to the school. This time, though, it wouldn't be about teacher turnover.

Not *exactly*, at least.

Come Friday afternoon, once the children had poured out of the building and only maintenance, administration, and overzealous teachers remained, Beverly bit the bullet.

She began at the cemetery, as she had the last time. The time when she'd sworn she'd never go back.

This was different, though. This visit had greater purpose. As such, Beverly parked in the lot just outside the black iron fence. Steeling herself, she pushed out of her car and strode quickly to the gates. She stood there a moment, beneath the black-smithed letters. *Harbor Hills Cemetery.* So simple. So hideous.

Then, she went in.

Anyone else would have to count the rows and columns to get there. Cousins. Aunts, uncles, and even best friends.

But not Kayla's mom.

Beverly could beeline to the gravestone, if she wanted. She didn't want to. She wanted to loiter. To inspect. To judge the upkeep. Eye the weeds. Silently curse the caretakers for not caring one iota.

In fact, they did care. At least, it looked that way. The weeds were cut low to blend in with the grass. Fresh flowers sprung out of stonewalled beds at the corners of each section of the ever-expanding lot of losses.

Try as she might, she could not find a single dandelion. Not one dry and crumpling leaf. No early signs of fall. Just perfection. Perfection amid tragedy.

Muscle memory and grief pulled Beverly like a magnet to Kayla's grave.

Her knees gave way and soon, she was on the grass, half sitting, half lying up to the marble slab. She traced Kayla's name, murmured it to herself. Whispered and wept and then pushed back to her knees, sitting on her calves and ignoring the pain of early middle age and a lack of exercise.

She wondered what she, as a mom, did wrong.

If Kayla were texting behind the wheel, then whose fault was that?

Tom's of course. He was in the *car* with her. And he *let* her.

Police records showed that final message. *Be there soon!*

The bitter irony crushed Beverly.

She pressed her hand to her mouth, then to Kayla's name.

With the kiss, Beverly absorbed the guilt. She breathed it in and held that breath for five beats.

Then, she stood and brushed grass blades from her knees and hip. She let out the breath and made a quiet promise. A promise to Kayla, and a promise to herself. She'd avenge this tragedy. She'd find out why in the *world* Tom Castle let their daughter use her cell phone while she was driving through winter weather. She'd rewrite history and throw all those awful newspaper stories back in the faces of the small-town reporters who were supposed to be on *her* side—Beverly's side. Their colleague's side.

She'd bury the headlines.

The bad ones: Teenage Texting Results in Death of Local Girl and Her Father.

The worse ones: Local Teacher and Daughter Dead. Cause? Texting while Driving.

And the worst one: Life of Young Local Lost to a Preventable Tragedy.

To his credit, Forrest hadn't permitted any callous coverage. All those headlines came from county reporters from sister towns.

And now, he'd have to let her make it all okay.

Beverly Castle would set the record straight.

But first, she needed a better headline. And she'd have to be more direct than Teacher

Turnover. Because even if the cause of this tragedy was folded into the skeletons of the high school, nobody cared about teachers and their turnover rates.

They didn't care about a mom trying to fix her dead daughter's damaged reputation.

They cared about high stakes at high school.

Lies during English Lessons.

Scandal in the School System.

And boy howdy, did Beverly Castle have a scandal for them.

"BEVERLY?"

She'd caught Darry Ruthenberg in the front hall-way, a Tupperware bowl in one hand, plastic spoon lifting to his mouth with the other.

Beverly grimaced and eyed the clock on the wall behind him. "Is that lunch or dinner?"

He lowered the spoon, his expression relaxing. "Both?"

"I wanted to talk. About my story? About the school?"

Darry glanced behind her, as if half expecting a ghost from the cemetery to appear, hovering over her shoulder. Maybe Kayla. Maybe Tom. Beverly was full of ghosts, she guessed.

"You're still doing the story?" he asked.

"I'm doing *a* story. A different one, I think. More about"—she blinked and sucked in a breath—"more about Kayla."

He set his lunch-dinner down on the nearby countertop then slid his hands into his pockets. "Whatever it is you need, Beverly, I can try to help. Just...don't slam us to the community. The school had nothing to do with the accident."

"I know that," she agreed.

"Then what do you need from the school? From *me*?"

"I need some basic information. That's all. I just —I have a hunch, Darry."

He frowned. "A hunch about what?"

"About Kayla and the school."

"The school had nothing to do with the accident," he repeated.

"I know that. But *the school* is the only way I can learn about Mrs. Spectre."

His jaw didn't drop. His eyes didn't widen. No reaction. This was worse than *a* reaction.

Beverly doubled down. "I need to dig around, Darry. I need answers."

"Whatever Spectre had to do with Kayla—or *Tom*—is not connected here." He pressed his hands down to emphasize their location.

"Sure, but I *know* she did something wrong. I just don't know what. And the only thing I can do is search her classroom. The school. The only place I can *possibly* get access to."

"I can't give you that kind of access. Not to staff or students. Not to the campus, Bev." He stopped and pushed both hands through his hair. At last, he righted himself and narrowed his eyes on Beverly. "But I can give you something else."

"What?"

His mouth stayed in a flat line, his eyes sad. But behind the blankness of his expression, Beverly saw something else in Darry as he said, "So long as it's off the record, I can give you *me*."

CHAPTER 20—ANNETTE

It had been two weeks since Annette and Roman had terminated their lease on Main Street. Two weeks of crowding each other's bubble around the clock at home. Despite each having his and her *own* in-home office space, it seemed as though Roman wandered in and out of Annette's dedicated room every fifteen minutes. Sometimes, he was "just looking for something!" Other times, he had "an important question" only to forget what it was. Some wives might find this sort of interruption endearing. Annette found it mainly annoying. Especially when she was answering client phone calls and Roman couldn't seem to take the hint when she glared at him and waved him out as a potential buyer blared forth from her phone speaker.

But now it was Saturday, and they were officially packing up those in-home offices in preparation for the big move.

Roman had drawn up the paperwork, and they'd met with Elora and Tad Beckett. Everything looked to be a go. They were just waiting on final inspections, set to take place the following week.

It was a whirlwind, the housing swap. For a while, Annette figured it wouldn't come true. Who could manage such a thing?

Turned out Roman could. This feat alone had overridden any of her annoyance at him. Still, though, it hadn't made the packing any less contentious.

The one fact that kept Annette from bawling about the move—really, she'd much rather stay put in her beautiful Apple Hill home—was the fact that she was hardly moving at all. She'd be half a stone's throw from her own backyard, in the house kitty-corner on Dogwood Drive.

After a summer of growing so attached to her neighbors—at long last—it'd be a travesty to tear away. From the friendship. The fun. And, now, the mystery of Carl Carlson. Annette was all in.

That's why, when Elijah invited Vivi over to help on Saturday, Annette decided to set up a little luncheon. It was her chance to pick away at the latest intrigues of 696. Anyway, she hadn't seen either Vivi or Quinn—or anyone else on the street—all week. They were all swept up in back to school. Normally, Annette would be, too. Not this year, though. This year, she was prepping for the move.

Vivi appeared at the front door late in the morning, after Annette had boxed the last of her china.

For the first time ever, Annette beat Elijah to the door. "Viviana!" she exclaimed. "So happy to have your help today."

Vivi, dressed in denim overalls with her white hair braided in two wispy plaits, reminded Annette of an ironic Elly May Clampett. It was interesting how Vivi dressed around Elijah versus how she dressed for nearly everything else. Generally, she appeared polished and stylish—effortlessly so. When she was at the Best house, her look transformed into something indescribable. Like she was testing the limits of her identity with Elijah. Annette found the experiment charming and telling, like together, the two could be themselves—and all that that entailed.

"No problem." Vivi beamed back. "Either I'm

working here or at home, and I'd rather be with Eli. I mean—" She flushed deeply, but Annette knew better than to react.

She waved. "I get it. Being with friends passes the time. Maybe you and I should swap? I could help Quinn over there, and you can take over for me here. Seems more interesting at your house, anyway."

Vivi stepped in and followed Annette to the kitchen. "More interesting?"

"All that stuff Beverly Castle was talking about at brunch last week. Remember? *Someone else lived there*," Annette said in a ghostly voice as she wriggled her eyebrows.

Vivi opened her mouth to reply but was swiftly cut off by Elijah, who'd barreled into the kitchen fresh out of the shower. A shower that would be best taken *after* cleaning...

"Kayla's mom got that idea from Kayla, you know," he said ominously.

Both Annette and Vivi turned to Elijah, their mouths falling open.

"What?" Annette demanded. "What do you mean she got the idea from Kayla?"

He shrugged like it was old news. "Kayla's dad *saw* someone there. At old man Carlson's." He glanced at Vivi. "At your house, I mean," he clarified by way of apology.

"Tom? When?" Annette pressed him.

"I guess when they first moved in. They wanted to buy *this* house—the Castles, I mean." He scrunched his face at Annette. "Mom, I thought you *knew* this."

"Knew *what*? That people shop around before buying a house?" Annette laughed in spite of herself, enraptured by the fact that her teenage son was ahead of the curve on neighborhood gossip.

"I dunno," he grumbled lamely, lifting an apple wedge from the plate Annette had set out. He dunked it into the ranch that was *meant* for the carrots then added, "I just mean, you know everything."

"Well, I didn't know Tom Castle had ever *seen* anyone."

"It was probably Jeanette, right?" Vivi offered. "The daughter?"

"It wouldn't have been Bernie and Irma's daughter," Annette reasoned. "Carl was here when the Castles moved onto the block, right?" The question was entirely rhetorical. She scratched beneath her hair at the back of her neck. "I thought so at least." Annette's eyes flashed to Vivi.

"Have you found anything? Anything other than the pendant?" She referenced the inscrutable charm—if you could call it that—that still hung around Vivi's neck.

Vivi and Elijah exchanged a look. "Nope," Vivi said, her gaze sliding away.

Annette studied her more closely, but the conversation rippled away like the tide.

"What do we need to do today, Mom?" Elijah asked, effectively undermining Annette's aims to draw out more information about her neighbor's predecessors.

"Oh, right." Annette let forth a sigh. She glanced around as the two shoveled her famous breakfast croissants down their gullets like they hadn't eaten in a week. Vivi wasn't afraid to dive into food around Elijah. Boxes took up corners of every room, the monumental task of packing their *real* everyday stuff looming heavily.

"What about linens?" Vivi asked, sounding very grown-up.

Annette shook her head. "No. I'm not sure what would be ready to go and what should stay." She crossed her arms and realized she was in that obnoxious position of needing help without knowing exactly *what* kind of help. Her eyes flicked through to the back window. Outside was as much an issue as inside. Between Roman's tools and—

"Hey," she said, pointing a clean fingernail—manicures had gone out with the rented office space.

Mouths full, Vivi and Elijah followed her finger. "What?" Eli asked after swallowing.

"I thought you finished the fort."

The fort in the backyard was less an eyesore than it was an attractive nuisance. Annette *and* Roman agreed it wasn't safe—not for the Becketts' young son or forthcoming twins. Better to tear it down than to bring it up to some kind of code, anyway.

When they'd bought the house, there had been a raised-bed garden in the farthest corner of the backyard. At ten-by-ten, it was the perfect size for a playhouse or a treehouse. Without a daughter and without a tree, though, thoughts of quaint, picture-perfect old-fashioned structures flew out the window. In their place, a good, old-fashioned, man-and-son-made fort. Out of scrap wood and even some hewed branches and logs from the forest's edge at the far back of Crabtree Court.

Elijah groaned. "We got as far as the lower wall and the floor. It's a lot of demo work, though. Dad added footers, remember?"

"Footers?" Annette slapped her forehead with

the palm of her hand. Typical Roman. Going above and beyond. Always. She grinned and shook her head good-humoredly.

"We'll need a pickax," Vivi added expertly.

"Is your mom okay with you handling a pickax?" Annette propped her hands on her hips.

Vivi shrugged. "I've handled much worse."

Sighing, Annette accepted defeat. "Okay. There's one in Dad's shed, E. Just...*be careful*."

CHAPTER 21—QUINN

Starting the second week of school had Quinn feeling a little more at ease.

This was due in large part to Vivi's enthusiastic overview of her school days. On Tuesday, she raved about how helpful Eli was. On Wednesday, she felt immediate connections with her teachers. On Thursday, she'd started making *other* friends. "Already!" she'd marveled. And on Friday, she'd learned that Homecoming was a "huge deal, Mom! Like, *major*." All of this worked well for Vivi, who was more social than either Quinn or Matt had ever been. Too social for Birch Harbor High, where the prevailing teenage attitude erred on the side of petulant, rather than peppy. Vivi needed peppy.

She'd needed it for a long time, probably. It was good for her.

But just as importantly as Vivi's newfound comfort was Quinn's. Quinn, too, had established some solid footing at the *Herald*.

The Monday after Labor Day, she was scheduled for a meeting with Forrest and Beverly to go over plans for rolling out Beverly's upcoming feature, which was supposed to be a big deal around the office.

The only problem was Beverly had been out of the picture on the home front. Her interest in Carl Carlson had all but bottomed out. At least so far as Quinn could tell.

Come meeting time on Monday, Beverly was a no-show.

At ten sharp, Forrest swung into Quinn's new office—a small room that used to be a copy room but was converted when they moved the machine into the back supply closet. "Seen Bev today?"

"Beverly?" Quinn glanced up from her computer. She'd been tweaking their Twitter bio. "Nope." She frowned then lifted a finger. "Well, I saw her around her house yesterday. I think. I mean I saw her car there, at least."

He looked toward the front of the office then back at her, bounced the butt of his hand against the door jamb a few times, then swung all the way into her office. "Whatcha up to?"

Quinn swiveled her monitor toward him.

"Riveting," he cracked before squinting and leaning in. His cologne rushed her nose. Curve? Couldn't be. That was so—dated. And yet so...*welcome*. Quinn became very aware of just how close to her he was. His still-damp curly hair gave off its own heady flavor—men's shampoo or gel. Fresh but virile.

Swallowing, she stole a glance from the corner of her eye, catching his freckles—a spray of auburn across his nose and up into his forehead. They gave way along his cheeks to a recently shaven jawline. Not too recent, though. Specks of razor-shorn chestnut beard poked through in patches. Imperceptible stubble and fine crow's-feet complemented the sophomoric smell of his cologne and just-out-of-the-shower hair. Everything worked together to result in an attractive proof of age, and Quinn felt strange to notice it all. Weird. Like a teenager with an out-of-reach crush.

Inwardly embarrassed, she leaned away and sank back into her chair. Forrest glanced at her then took the hint she didn't mean to drop, and he pushed back a few inches too. Still, he read the draft copy aloud. "The *Harbor Herald* newspaper covers Michigan's Harbor Hills, serving the greater Birch Harbor area. Follow us for local, late-breaking news." He nodded mock seriously at her. "Perfect."

"Thanks." She smiled back easily, then caught herself and wiped her mouth with the back of her hand like she'd had a milk mustache. "Should we go ahead and have the meeting? Without Beverly?"

He smirked. "Beverly is *running* the meeting. It's her story. We're just support systems."

He dropped into the spare chair across from her desk. The small space shrank further now, and Quinn felt her neck flush with heat. She wiped her mouth again. And a third time. Then her leg got to bouncing beneath her desk.

She asked, "Well, if we know she's moving ahead with the Carlson piece, we can work with that. We don't have to have the whole story to make a game plan, right? And anyway, why *are* we meeting exactly?" This was an earnest question. Quinn didn't know all that much about newspaper operations yet, but Forrest had been treating the Carlson story like a movie premiere. They'd offered interviews with sister publications and bought ad space for the paper on social media and in the *Coffee News*. Things that Forrest Jericho had never done in his tenure as editor, according to *him*.

"Sorry!" came a cry from the clattering front door. Bells went off and wood hit wood twice as the owner of the voice got the door to shut firmly—always a challenge in the humid months, according, again, to Forrest.

He whipped around and leaned back in his chair, and Quinn's eyes fell down his torso to where his pants fabric creased at the crotch. She quickly looked away, humiliated at her own indecency.

"Bev!" Forrest called out, oblivious to Quinn's licentious ogle. "We're in here!"

He stood and pulled the chair out, pressing his body against the wall nearest Quinn. There were no opposing teams at the *Harbor Herald*. But it felt like he had just taken Quinn's side against Beverly, somehow.

But of course Quinn had it all wrong, and as Beverly stomped in with an air of exuberance and determination, any feeling of *us against them* dissipated. They were once again a team. Professionals. Coworkers.

Quinn's office space returned to its original size,

the heat lifted, and Quinn was once again an inconsequential newbie.

Beverly beamed at both of them, but she didn't sit down. Didn't drop her satchel. She stood in the doorway. "There's been a change in plans."

CHAPTER 22—BEVERLY

Once Darry had agreed to talk, the game was *on*. He'd had plans Friday and Saturday—family in town. So, they had parted ways with a promise to meet Monday morning in his office—*off* the record.

He had only half an hour to give her—in between morning bus duty and a district admin meeting upstairs. She took what she could get and showed up early, ready and raring.

Darry didn't waste time. At exactly nine, he had appeared in the waiting area by the front desk and gestured her back to his office. She'd followed without hesitation and they'd cracked into her list of questions.

"Why did Kayla have Christie Spectre's phone number?"

He didn't know.

"Why was Kayla going to Christie Spectre's house the night of the accident?"

He didn't know.

"What was Kayla's grade in Mrs. Spectre's class up to the night of her passing?"

This had taken some computer navigation, but he found it, answering, at last, reluctantly. "A C."

"A *C*?" Beverly had been shocked. "Kayla never got a C in her life."

He shrugged and rotated the computer screen to prove it. Her progress report for the grading period in question indeed showed *C. Spectre—Honors English 9—78%*.

"Did Tom run an after-school club?"

His eyes had flashed at her at that one, but it wasn't exactly a guilty look, no.

"No, Bev," he'd answered quietly. "Nothing *official*, at least."

She'd kept stoic, nodding and jotting it down like a simple fact of minimal interest. Inside, though, Beverly knew that this was the catch. The moment. Tom had told Beverly he was running Creative Writing

Club. Prior to the accident, she'd never thought to question it. Tom was a joiner. He'd be a club sponsor, of course he would. That was Tom. And anyway, she could have easily cross-checked with Kayla.

But she never did. And Kayla was a math-science kid, anyway. Even if there was a creative writing club, it'd fly under her radar. Doubly so if her *father* ran it.

She'd bitten her lip and lifted her gaze to Darry. The last question hung between her parted lips, but she never did get a chance to ask.

A phone call had come in for Darry. He'd had to take it. But as she had pushed up to excuse herself, he'd mouthed something to her. *I'll text you.*

CONVINCING her editor that she could handle this new story was the next hurdle.

She stood in the doorway to Quinn's office, hoping to use her neighbor and friend as leverage.

Forrest eyed her. "What's the change?" He looked at Quinn, who shrugged.

Beverly set her jaw and nodded slowly, eyeing Quinn all the while. "Well, you know, we *met* about Quinn's house. I met with Quinn and my mom—my two main sources. Quinn knows." Beverly crinkled her brows at Quinn. "Right?"

Quinn looked like a deer in headlights. It was clear she could tell she was about to be roped into taking a side, and it was clear that she understood the ramifications of such a position.

Beverly didn't want to pin anyone against anyone else, but she needed all the ammo she could get to convince Forrest that she was up to the task she was about to drop on him.

At last, Quinn turned her head to Forrest then shrugged. "I mean...we haven't talked about it since that brunch—"

"Because there's nothing to talk about," Beverly rushed to add.

"There's plenty to talk about, though," Forrest argued, crossing his arms over his chest. "You said so yourself." He cocked his head, and this was the moment that Beverly knew that *he* knew.

"Forrest, I have to do this."

He shook his head. "We agreed. You can't, Bev." He looked down at Quinn. "She can't."

"Can't what?" Quinn looked confused. "Go back to the teacher story?"

"Yes," Forrest answered, "because Beverly was never going to write about teacher turnover like we planned. She was taking it in a different direction." His gaze was steel, his jaw muscles clenched. "You can't go there, Bev. Let the dead stay dead."

Beverly's gut twisted. "I'll do the teacher turnover story, too. I'll write about the school in the same story. But I am doing this. You don't have to publish it if you don't want to."

"Then why do it if I won't publish it?" They were speaking the same language now.

Beverly replied, fiery. "I'll find another paper who will." She set her stare on him, and it was like Quinn had disappeared from the room.

Now, cousin-to-cousin, Forrest saw the truth. He had to give. He had no choice. This had just elevated from a work matter...to a family matter.

"Beverly, when we talked about the piece, you agreed—it was a continuation of our public schools series. Teacher turnover. *That* was the drama. You've now pivoted from dramatic territory into dangerous territory. Whatever it is you think you want to know..." He trailed off, unable to further justify his stance.

Beverly hitched her satchel up higher on her shoulder. "I just need a title, and you can start your promotions. Give me the morning to think it over, and I'll share it."

"I want a turnover piece," Forrest warned. "Something family friendly but stimulating. Something *inspirational* but *provocative*. Something to quench the need for small-town gossip in a productive way and that digs around in the bowels of the school. All of that. In one pat little piece *without* you airing your personal problems to the world. Got it?"

"Fine."

She left Quinn's office and made her way to her own. Once she was there, her phone buzzed in her satchel. Beverly pulled it out to see a text from Darry.

Let's get together to talk. How's next Saturday? 6pm at Eat Street...?

An inappropriate elation sparked inside her. Inappropriate in that, since the winter before, Beverly had assumed there was nothing in life that could possibly stir up feelings of hope or happiness. Not information on her dead family. And certainly not dinner out with Darry Ruthenberg, her high school boyfriend.

But Forrest was right. Beverly didn't *want* to know about Tom and Kayla and Christie Spectre.

She *had* to know.

CHAPTER 23—JUDE

L ate September had officially arrived. The twenty-second, to be specific. A Day One, so far as Mother Nature was concerned.

This made Jude antsy. In her adult life, she'd been a summer girl. Boating and backyard brunches. Of course, Gene and Jude would celebrate the other seasons, too. But they were a summer couple. Which meant, come autumn, the decorations came down along with the pretenses. They'd stow away in Gene's car, doing a loop around the state and coming back home to Harbor Hills until the next long weekend, when they'd take off again. When Jude was with Gene, she'd still been responsible for hanging the cobwebs for Halloween and the Christmas lights for Christmas. For New Year's, they'd host an extravagant party on the Birch Harbor marina, if they weren't already committed to someone else's yacht or lakefront mansion, that is. When it was Valentine's Day, she'd cut out paper hearts and pin them to the fridge with magnets only to be overshadowed by Gene's grandiose gestures of romance—champagne and dinner reservations and roses, maybe jewelry, too. Over the top and insincere. Always.

Now that they weren't together, Jude was free of all that. After all, she had only ever been one to decorate and revel at her ex-husband's behest. Not at her own. And doing so would dredge up not only memories of Gene and their put-on marriage, but childhood memories, too. Unfond ones, at that. Opposite types of memories. It was as though the pendulum, for Jude, had swung far to the other side with marriage. Now, it'd swung right back to where it began. In that origin of pain.

Wednesday, after school, she'd scheduled a distraction. While her neighbors were plucking the miniature American flags from the soft soil by their mailboxes and pruning back dead and dying sunflowers, Jude would be courting a consultation on her home reno plans.

She pulled back the lace curtains that dangled

by the front window and peered up the street, looking for his truck.

Instead, Jude saw Quinn and Vivi at the bottom of their driveway. Quinn staked a bamboo-and-straw scarecrow into the patch of grass that abutted the sidewalk. Vivi stood back and appeared to study it. In her own hand dangled a second scarecrow, this one smaller. After a moment, Quinn and Vivi had successfully propped both scarecrows together, one just in front of the other, like diminutives of the mother-daughter duo.

Red flashed at the top of the street, snapping Jude to attention. She swallowed and pushed her hair up in the back then gave one last look around, ensuring the house was tidy.

Within ninety seconds, he was at the door, ringing the bell, sending a jolt through Jude's nervous system and flutters to her chest.

She counted to five, smoothed her peach-colored shift dress, and opened the door with a put-on air of surprise and, of course, a wide smile.

To the visitor, Jude beamed. "Hi!"

"Hi!" Dean Jericho beamed back.

THE NEXT DAY, Jude floated into her classroom. This was ridiculous, of course. As if! As if talk of dry wall and paint and new light fixtures was *titillating*. It wasn't. Not normally.

But chatting with Dean Jericho had spurred something in Jude. Maybe it was oppositeness to Gene. Or his kind eyes, crinkly and age appropriate. Free of Botox and tanning spray.

So un-Gene. So delectable.

Or maybe it was the fact that Dean's arrival to Chateau Banks was the start of something. Not romantic, no. Something for Jude. A new chapter. Or even a whole new book!

Between the changes in her heart and in her house, showing up to Hills High on that second day of autumn on the fourth day of the third week of school...*oh*! Everything felt *right*.

Until, during lunch, a face appeared in her classroom window—the one that looked out onto the lawn that stretched between the school building and the visitor parking lot.

A familiar face.

"Beverly?" Jude twisted the name on her tongue, confused by the apparition-like figure on the other side of the glass.

Beverly mouthed *Hi*, her lips alive with the sort

of energy that had carried Jude forward that very morning.

Jude shook her head, mouthing back, *What are you doing here?*

Beverly pointed westward, indicating a teacher-access door on the side of the building.

Jude clued in and hurried to the door, her to-go salad in one hand.

She pushed it open, looking behind her, unsure about this. "Is everything okay?" she half whispered to Beverly, who took a step into the darkened end of the hall, joining Jude. Was this illegal? Weren't visitors supposed to sign in?

"Sorry to sneak in like this," Beverly answered, looking past Jude and up the hall. "I wanted to see if you were free to have lunch!"

"Um..." Jude chewed her bottom lip. "I'd love to —but—"

"I'll go sign in," Beverly assured her, walking up the hall like she owned the place.

Jude followed, her teacher clogs thudding lightly on the tiled floor.

As promised, Beverly beelined for the front desk, greeting the receptionist easily and finishing her name with a flourish. Soon enough, they were back in Jude's classroom, undetected, more or less, by anyone who mattered.

"So," Jude started, "why the sneaky drop-in?" She laughed as lightly as possible, but the accusation in her words came through crystal clear.

Beverly shrugged. "What do you mean? I'm a stakeholder. I can be here." She said it with such contrived smugness that Jude had to laugh.

"Ah, yes. Public school, where *everyone* is a stakeholder." It sounded like a children's storybook. An uplifting story of community members pitching in at the local schoolhouse. Beverly seemed all too aware of this nuance.

"In all honestly, I'm avoiding Darry. He doesn't want me here." Beverly said it frankly, her face falling into something unreadable.

Jude gave her a look. "And why is that?" Then she lowered her face and her voice. "Are you doing that story on the school after all?" Jude's eyes grew wide.

Beverly nodded slowly. "Sort of."

Smiling, Jude returned to her classroom door, hesitated a moment, then—with the fortitude only a true friendship might inspire—she closed it and pressed herself against the wood. "Oh, my gosh. You're going to get me into trouble, aren't you?"

CHAPTER 24—BEVERLY

What she was doing wasn't *wrong*. Beverly was meeting her friend for lunch. She'd signed her name into the visitors' log. She'd made small talk with Miss Elaine. Everything was above board.

She'd even packed a turkey sandwich, apple slices, and two fresh-baked chocolate chip cookies to share with Jude. This was the exact lunch Beverly used to pack for Kayla—back when Kayla brought a sack lunch. Fixing it that very morning had been less emotional than Beverly had expected, largely because it was a rote procedure. Muscle memory took over, and the whole routine became something of a therapy.

Now, she popped open the Tupperware rectangle

inside of which awaited the cookies. Offering one to Jude, she finally came clean. "Have you found anything here?"

Jude, who'd settled into comfortable small talk with Beverly, now looked surprised. "Found anything?" She raised one eyebrow.

Beverly looked around the room, taking it all in. Nothing was familiar about it. Nothing at all. To Beverly, it now appeared as just another high school English classroom. Dated chalkboards clashed up against newer whiteboards. Inspirational posters, alternated with informational grammar posters, lined the wall space. A neat agenda was scrawled in careful cursive across the left side of the central whiteboard.

At last, she let out a slow breath. "The teacher who was in this room before you—I, um…" Beverly realized she hadn't exactly practiced what she'd say to Jude. Unlike any true local, Jude wouldn't be in the loop on Hills High drama. Or was she…? "Do you know who Christie Spectre is?"

Jude's eyes lit up. "Oh, sure. She left half her life here." Jude waved a hand back toward a closed door. A closet, maybe?

Beverly licked her lips. "She *did*?"

"Where is this going?" Jude leaned back a hair,

crossing one leg over the other and clasping her hands around her knee.

Beverly backtracked. "Christie Spectre was..." Swallowing, she wondered if she could come out with it. The feeling in her gut. The hope that there was *more* to the worst story ever. The truth would be best. Beverly locked eyes with Jude. "Christie Spectre is the person Kayla texted when she crashed. When she *died*."

THE SEARCH WAS LIKE A FEVER. Both women ripping through files and folders, binders and books, looking for something—anything to prove Christie Spectre had done something bad. It's what Beverly needed. She needed to share the guilt. The blame. And she needed to share it with someone living. God knew if Tom was alive, it'd be him she could scream to. She could shake him and kick at him and shove him around and *scream*.

But Tom was dead, too. And there had to be more to the story.

Beverly didn't realize it, not completely, but she was starting to question *everything*. She questioned if Kayla really was texting. And if so, why? Why couldn't it wait? And shouldn't the other person have known, somehow, that Kayla was *driving*? And it was Christie Spectre—why in the world did she have Kayla's phone number? There had to be a school policy against such a thing, right? Tom didn't text any of his students, did he?

Then again, that was where the line of questions skidded to a halt.

The ultimate question...the question that could both fix everything and ruin it in one fell swoop... was just that: what didn't Beverly know about her own husband?

And why did she have a hunch that Christie Spectre was part of the puzzle?

At one point in their shuffle in the closet, Jude stopped and stood up. "What am I looking for, Beverly?" she asked. It was the obvious question. And of course, Beverly didn't have an answer. Not a real one. "And why didn't Christie take this stuff with her? Lesson plans and unit plans. Worksheets and tests—surely she'd want all that at her next job?"

Beverly froze. She was hunched over a banker's box of alphabetized files. She looked up at Jude. "Only if she's teaching again."

"Why wouldn't she teach?"

"If she couldn't get a teaching job," Beverly replied.

Jude lowered to the floor, bracing herself with just her fingertips. The two women were inches apart, their breath heavy in the narrow space. "And why wouldn't she be able to get a teaching job?"

They answered together, word for word. A jinx, of sorts. "She got in trouble."

CHAPTER 25—ANNETTE

Tuesday, Annette was supposed to host the monthly HOA meeting at her house. She found this to be inconvenient, of course, what with half the house boxed now. Or a third of it, anyway.

So, she called Quinn. "Please," Annette begged that morning. "I'll do *everything*. I wasn't thinking when I agreed to host this time. I'll clean. I'll prep. Just tell me where your spare key is."

Quinn was at work, and Annette had no client appointments that day. Roman was covering everything from his home office, and it was for the best that the two spend a bit of time apart. They'd been encroaching on each other's spaces far too regularly, of late.

Quinn replied, "Vivi has it." She gasped. "Wait! The kids have a half day, right?"

"I can come to your office—" Annette started. "But yes!" School got out at one for parent-teacher conferences. Annette glanced at her watch. It was just after eleven. She could easily wait.

"Will she mind?" Annette asked. "Will *you* mind? If I head over and set up?"

"Not at all," Quinn answered. "But um—just avoid the garage if possible." A nervous chuckle followed, but Annette brushed it off. Typical female fear of judgment.

"No problem. I'll stick to the kitchen and...back porch?" Annette changed her mind. "Might be too cold. The meeting's at five." Another thought seized her. "Wait. Parent-teacher conferences...are any of the HOA board members parents? Or even teachers?" She did a quick calculation in her head. "No... just you and Jude, I think."

"And you," Quinn pointed out.

"I'll send Roman to the conference. With Eli, they're a breeze." She froze at the flippant comment. Maybe conferences weren't easy with Vivi. Annette didn't want to be a braggart. She added, "You know —*boys*," to smooth out any perception of a jab.

Quinn seemed not to notice, but she did fret. "I

have to go. Matt can't come to town tonight. And I'm not sure Vivi's will be so easy." Then she laughed. "You know—*girls*."

Annette smiled on her end of the line.

A COUPLE OF HOURS LATER, Elijah arrived home. This was Annette's prompt. "Hey!" She slid him a plate of sliced apples arranged around a dish of melted caramel—a practice round for that evening. "I need to go over to Quinn's and prep for the HOA thing tonight. Wanna come?"

"Oh, um, Vivi was going to come over here. We have more to do outside, and since we have all afternoon..."

Annette leaned right and twisted, peering out through the back window. "For spending so much time out there, it seems like progress is a little slow." She lowered her chin and gave her son a look. "What *have* you two been doing?"

"Mom." Elijah glowered at her. But he flushed red, too, and blinked fast, one of his childhood tics rearing its head.

Annette held up her hands in surrender and averted her gaze, uncomfortable to be the source of her teenage son's discomfort. "Okay! Sorry! Never mind!" After a beat she added, "How about you two help me with the HOA setup over here? Could be a nice break from packing and cleaning, right?"

IN THE END, it took nothing at all to convince Elijah to go to Quinn's. After all, Vivi was there, and it turned out they hadn't made firm plans about working on the fort or packing Roman's tools *yet*.

Vivi showed Annette to the kitchen, pointing out leftovers in the fridge and clipped bags of popcorn and pretzels, twisted down to half their capacities. Annette already knew she'd need to bring in all food and drink, but Quinn's cupboards held more than enough paper products and plastic tumblers to host a town-wide party. Once the kids went upstairs—*homework*—Annette poked around in the built-in china cabinet, discovering dust-coated crystal stemware, mottled-glass punch bowls, and blue patterned serving plates by the dozen.

Clearly, the entire casement represented just a fraction of what Quinn had kept in the wake of Carl Carlson's departure. What Annette did not realize was the extent to which Quinn had saved some of his hoard. Interesting.

She sorted through the lot, selecting one plate for fruit and caramel, one for veggies and dip, and one for crackers and cheese—HOA meeting staples. After, she decided to wash up some of the goblets to use as drinking vessels, instead of the paper and plastic products.

Laughter trickled down the stairs, calling Annette to the foyer to stand there and contemplate going up.

More came and floated off. Pure and innocent. Because she could hear it so vividly, Annette assumed Vivi's door was ajar. Maybe even wide open. This is what she and Roman had taught Elijah. Maybe Quinn had the same rule. Regardless, nothing nefarious could possibly be underway with such childlike joy spilling from the second floor.

Annette swiveled around and studied the foyer, where the HOA would gather to remove any coats or hats or purses. A skeletal coat stand loomed in the corner by the door. On it, nothing. Not yet, of course. Quinn and Vivi hadn't lived in Harbor Hills through the cold season. They hadn't had the time to let years' worth of jackets and beanies and scarves accumulate.

Perfect.

Quinn yanked open the half door hidden along the inside of the staircase. Just as she expected—a store of cleaning equipment. She grabbed the hand vac and worked on the corners of the foyer and dining room. Then returned to the little cubby for the broom and dustpan to do a quick once-over of any exposed wood flooring.

After, she dug through all of the drawers in the kitchen and dining room—the cabinets—until she found a pretty beige tablecloth, which she was happy to find clean and relatively wrinkle free. With a touch of olive oil from the pantry and a rag from the dishcloth drawer, she rubbed the dining room table until it shone then wiped it with a clean towel to pull the excess oil. After cleaning the dishware first, she returned to the table, which was now dry, shook the covering out, and let it flutter perfectly down, covering the table just enough.

Satisfied, Annette tidied the kitchen and returned to the base of the staircase.

The laughter didn't come. Only silence from above.

She mounted the first step. Waited. Listened.

Nothing still.

Surely the kids hadn't come downstairs. She'd have noticed them.

Annette took the second step.

Waited. Listened.

Still, nothing.

She glanced at her watch, like the timepiece might have some answer. It did not.

She took the third step, then pushed the rest of the way up, landing on tiptoes at the carpeted hallway above.

Annette had never been to the second floor of Carl Carlson's—er, Quinn's—house. Even when helping with the yard sale from that summer, she'd been relegated to the downstairs. She didn't know which bedroom was Quinn's or Vivi's or if there was an office...a guest room...

She tested her weight on the runner. Indeed, the wooden planks beneath it creaked to life.

Wincing, she settled carefully then looked to her left. The bedroom door there was ajar. Inside, a four-poster queen bed with a messy down comforter stood clearly empty. Quinn's room.

Directly in front of Annette, another door. This one shut. She hazarded another creaking pace toward the door and listened.

This time, she heard murmurs, although they

didn't sound like they were coming from within the room in front of her. She leaned forward and pressed the side of her head against the wood. Another ripple of human voices but more muted now. Annette felt ridiculous. She gave one swift knock then twisted the doorknob and swung into the room.

Empty. Save for dated furniture.

Turning on a heel, she pulled the door closed and made for the right side of the hall.

Indeed, the hum of teenagers grew louder. Annette realized that if she just walked normally her own sounds faded into white noise. She passed a bathroom, white-and-black-tiled with a clawfoot tub, much like the one in her own house.

Beyond that, another door. This one cracked.

Relief filled Annette's chest.

She now stood just in front of the door. Annette knew better than to embarrass Elijah. But she was already here and now even more curious than when she thought they might be up to no good.

"Knock-knock!" she trilled gently, gripping the edge of the door and poking in. She'd regret this. In fact, as soon as she saw their feet dangling off the edge of Vivi's bed, she regretted it.

Both their faces whipped around in panic.

Annette clenched her hands into fists and took a single step back. "Sorry, you two. I—"

"Mom." Elijah sat up. "Come here."

Awkwardly, Annette padded forward into the room, trying to look anywhere but at Elijah and Vivi, who were sprawled comfortably on their stomachs on the bed.

But then— "Did you know about this?"

She cleared her throat, licked her lips, and tried for a smile. As her gaze settled back on them, she realized there really wasn't anything clandestine or scandalous underway on Vivi's bed, despite the fact that, well, the two were *lying* on her bed. This alone, in Annette's mind, was an indecent position. She tried hard to ignore her motherly instinct to force them into separate chairs.

"Know about what?" she managed, her smile straining every moment that passed and they remained in their relaxed, informal, over-friendly pose.

At that, Elijah pushed up, and Annette finally saw that it wasn't anything untoward that had their attention.

Vivi sat up, too, her eyes fiery.

Annette joined them at the bed, lowering so that all three were now on Vivi's quilt.

Elijah swiveled his laptop so Annette could see it, and Vivi reached toward her desk, plucking a newspaper from the edge. "Mrs. Castle wrote this article about a missing Detroit woman who was connected to Harbor Hills. Do you remember this case?"

Annette rolled her eyes. "Eli," she said, standing from the bed and folding her arms, "if you have extra time, we are at the one-month-out marker."

"One month until what?" Vivi piped up.

"Until we move," Elijah grumbled.

"Oh, right."

Annette smiled at both. "And no. I don't remember that story." She flipped her brown hair back with a hand and started for the door. "And if there *was* a missing woman who just so happened to be *connected* to Harbor Hills and went missing around the same time we moved here, I think I'd remember." She smirked. "In fact, we probably wouldn't have *moved* here."

But privately Annette knew that was a fib. Of course something like a missing woman wouldn't turn her off of a town. Quite the opposite. For a woman like Annette, a story-chaser in her own right, well, she'd have tracked down that woman herself.

CHAPTER 26—QUINN

Quinn returned from Vivi's parent-teacher conference surprisingly chipper.

She'd steeled herself for the worst. Luckily, though, all the teachers and even the principal himself had awarded Viviana Fiorillo glowing reviews. They'd selected words like *attentive. Very smart.* Quinn flushed when she found herself in Jude Banks's classroom.

"You've got a lot to be proud of in Vivi, Quinn," Jude had assured her. "She focuses on her schoolwork. She's well liked. And she seems to, well, like it here. A lot. She seems—*happy.*"

With that, Quinn had floated home, forgetting entirely that Annette had come by to spruce things up for the HOA meeting. Forgetting, too, that an HOA meeting was set to commence in her own dining room.

When she arrived back home, her good mood twisted into confusion. Four unfamiliar cars were parked outside. The front porch light glowed softly as evening took hold of Apple Hill Lane.

Then she remembered.

Quinn tapped her fingers against the steering wheel in the perfunctory pattern of the alphabet on a QWERTY keyboard—a holdover habit from when she took a typing class in high school. She then stalled at the bottom of the driveway. It was awkward entering her own home...late. Like this.

She pulled her phone out to see if Vivi was hiding in her room or partaking of the neighborly festivities, her left eye twitching from exhaustion and her left knee bobbing compulsively as she took three deep breaths and awaited her daughter's response.

Vivi replied right away. *At E's!*

Quinn chewed over her options. Enter the HOA meeting and draw attention—potentially have the opportunity to gush over her amazing daughter. *Or* go directly to said amazing daughter and gush *to* her.

Her knee stopped bobbing, her eye stopped

twitching, and she rolled past her own driveway and into Annette's.

THEY WERE SITTING cross-legged on the sofa, a laptop open in Elijah's lap as Vivi leaned into him, reading over his shoulder.

"But she was from here," Elijah argued.

"Who was from here?" Quinn dropped her keys into her purse and lowered to the armchair adjacent.

Elijah looked up first. "Hi, Mrs. Whittle." He had a sort of Opie look about him. Thin-limbed and lanky and brown puppy-dog eyes. Downy brown hair swept neatly into an old-fashioned boy's style. He was anything but Vivi's type, assuming a teenage girl could even have a type. But he was cute. You could tell he'd grow up to be handsome. Above both of those, of course, Eli was a smart boy and a very nice one. The things that mattered.

"Mom." Vivi's eyes lit up. This was Excited Vivi. The sort of Vivi who filled a room with energy. Who had patience for her mom, and affection, too. "We're onto something."

"Oh, really?" It felt like they'd sailed back in time, when Vivi was much younger and had one of her Great Ideas. But, so, too, did Quinn have big news. "I have something to share myself."

Vivi's expression twitched, and she moved away from Elijah. "Oh, right. Conferences?" She squeaked through the one-word question.

"Vivi." Quinn beamed. "Who *are* you?"

Elijah lifted his eyes from his computer again, this time shifting them between Vivi and Quinn as if steeling himself for conflict.

But Vivi was Excited Vivi right now, and she rolled her eyes playfully, nudging Eli in the shoulder as if they shared a secret.

Maybe they did.

"Well, let me just say that the teachers raved about you." She winked at Vivi, and for a moment, Vivi's face reddened and her cheeks lifted. She was proud. Good. Quinn looked then at Elijah. "I saw your dad. He was just getting there as I was leaving, I think."

Elijah nodded then turned his computer for Quinn to see before nodding to Vivi.

Vivi explained. "When we had the yard sale, we found this article Beverly Castle wrote." She produced a folded-up square of newsprint, unfolding it as she passed it to Quinn.

Quinn studied the yellowed page. "Where'd you

get this?"

"In one of Carl's stacks." Lately, they'd taken to referring to Carl Carlson as just Carl, as if they knew him.

"He saved this on purpose?"

Elijah shook his head. "I don't think so. It was just in a stack with every other paper."

"But at the top," Vivi pointed out.

Quinn returned her stare to the page. "Okay, and so?" She scanned the article.

"It's like a *local* unsolved mystery," Vivi replied. "So cool."

"Temperance Temper." The name was only vaguely familiar to Quinn. But *recently* familiar. Had she seen a story in the annals of social media at the office? No. She shrugged. "Very cool." After half a beat, she added, "I guess."

"Anyway, we're going to track her down." Vivi squeezed Eli's arm eagerly. "Aren't we, Eli?"

Quinn stood to head home. She never felt entirely comfortable with teenagers. Maybe that had to do with her own youth. "Track who down?"

"Temperance Temper," Vivi replied simply, her eyes again glued to Elijah's screen. Who knew what was back there? After all, how far could such a case really go in the rabbit hole of the internet? Some old-timey gal lost in rural Michigan? Not too far from a *lake*, mind you.

As if reading her mind, Elijah closed the laptop and glanced at Vivi then at Quinn. "We've exhausted our resources. Read everything to read and gotten nowhere. There has to be more, though. Should we hit the library next?"

Yes, but Quinn had a better idea first. "Why not go directly to the source?"

"The source?" Elijah asked.

It was Vivi, though—smart girl that she was— who put it together. "Oh, my gosh, *duh*!" She grabbed Elijah's arm again. "Beverly! Let's talk to Beverly Castle!"

CHAPTER 27—BEVERLY

A sharp knock stirred Beverly awake on Saturday morning.

She'd fallen asleep on the sofa. Medically induced coma, she'd called these episodes. Fully dressed, fully makeupped, and fully full of one each: her Ambien, her Xanax, and one dangerously topped-off glass of Moscato. A precarious combination for anyone.

The knock discombobulated her. Then again, she was already discombobulated from her bad choices—the meds and the drink. Stupid. Stupid but necessary the night prior. After a whirlwind two weeks of tracking down leads on Christie Spectre, she'd hit a wall. Friday, she couldn't sleep. Unmoored by the anticipation of Saturday's meeting with Darry, she'd let herself succumb to the evils of substance.

Squinting around the living room, one hand pressed to the side of her head to subdue an oncoming crush of a headache, she tried to get her bearings.

Firstly, she realized she was *in* her living room. That was a starting point.

Next, she realized it was late. The sunrise that typically blasted through the living room windows was nowhere to be seen. Higher up than her house by now.

She pushed up slowly, squeezing her eyes shut and silently cursing herself for not stopping at *just* an Ambien. Or *just* a Xanax. *Just* one glass of wine.

Another rap. This one dragged Beverly's groggy attention to the front door.

Right.

But wait, what if it was *really* late? What if it was Darry at the door? Picking her up for their meeting? He'd leave, no doubt. She'd be fired, no doubt. People would talk, no doubt!

Beverly dropped back to the sofa, covering her face in a pillow and probably smearing her mascara even worse. Whoever it was would go away if she just waited them out. Most people could take a hint.

Then, once the coast was clear, she'd chug a carafe of coffee, shower, shave, and take a fresh, non-medically induced nap—assuming it wasn't late afternoon already.

The doorbell chimed—hers was a faint doorbell, courtesy of Tom, who hated for the dogs to get riled.

The dogs, yes. Beverly peeked out from beneath her pillow. Sandy and Danny lay in a near perfect yin-yang, long since *over* the visitor. Ever since Tom and Kayla died, the dogs had lost their protective nature, apparently. They'd become ghosts. Reminders of Kayla's favorite musical, *Grease*.

Beverly's gut clenched, but she took a deep breath and the feeling passed.

Whew.

After the doorbell, the knocking returned.

"Oh, good gracious," Beverly muttered, sitting back up and leaning forward to peer through the edge of the window. She might get a peek.

Just as she caught the edge of a view of the front porch, a face appeared there—or the slit of a face. Then a hand, waving, apparently.

Next came her name. "Mrs. Castle!" Loud on the porch, probably. Hollering. But muted and muffled to Beverly.

It was definitely not Darry, so she rocked up off

the sofa. Only then did Sandy and Danny stir. Confused like Beverly.

Beverly rubbed beneath her eyes and worked her jaw then shook out her hair. She peered through the peephole and two teenagers came into focus.

She gave it a moment's consideration before opening the door.

"Mrs. Castle!" Vivi cried triumphantly. "We *knew* you were home."

"Thought you might be dead, though," Elijah added. It was meant as a joke. Of course it was. Still, his face turned beet red. Blood vessels on his neck protruded. He looked like he was choking on shame. "I just mean that we've come by every day this week, and you haven't answered yet, but today we—" he flushed deeper. "Never mind."

Beverly sighed and tried for a smile. "It's been a long week, but I'm alive and well, actually. I'm a little worse for wear, though." She studied them momentarily. "You want to come in?"

They nodded eagerly.

She patted her hair and waved a hand back. "Welcome to Castle *Castle*," she said with a wry smile and deep voice.

"Heh. It's a dad joke, sort of," Vivi answered.

They followed Beverly to the living room, where

the dogs sniffed the newcomers and Beverly tidied up her makeshift bed. "Tom coined the phrase. 'Castle *Castle*,' he'd say with this grandiose British accent. He was good at the accent, too." A pain struck her heart, but Beverly was getting better at tamping that down. Especially since her assumptions were coming together.

"I know," Elijah murmured.

Beverly eyed him. "You know?"

"Mr. Castle would call his classroom that, too. 'Castle *Castle*.' Like it was Castle... I don't know. Like Castle Dracula or something." He glowed with the memory. Smiled and *glowed*.

Beverly swallowed. "He was your English teacher." It was one of those little aftershocks. The soft and sweet kind that tickled her chest and pushed her mouth up and crinkled her eyes.

"He was a really good teacher." Elijah all but whispered it, his head down, eyes on the striped rug. Tom would have hated the rug. She'd found it on clearance at a boutique in Birch Harbor just that month. Summer sale. It was a summery rug. Nautical with its blue and white color blocks running perpendicular to the sofa.

Vivi made a sound with her mouth. "I have Ms. Banks this year. For English, I mean." She grimaced.

"Sorry—I'm not trying to...steal the conversation." Then, she looked thoughtful. "Did she re—" She struggled over the word.

"Jude replaced Mrs. Spectre *and* Tom. I think they probably keep his classroom closed. You're in Christie's old classroom." Beverly sorted a stack of pages on the coffee table, tapping them on the wood to even them out. It was the contents of one of the manila folders in Jude's closet—Christie's closet.

Her answer was met with a brief silence. Beverly lay the stack of papers down. "Is that why you came by? To talk about the high school?" Her interest tingled. Maybe they had more information for her, and they were about to share it. Maybe kids and teachers were talking.

"Oh, no." Vivi sat up straighter, her ponytail flipping over the top of her head. The return of eighties fashion hit Beverly with warmth. Her childhood— Jellies, *Care Bears* on the console television, and a crusty orange sofa in the B&B—now felt like a dream too good to be true. Would she go back if she could? Not marry Tom? Not ever have Kayla? Beverly had heard that you can't lose something you never had.

Then again, you can't have something if you never lose.

And Beverly had *something*. She had her daughter.

She blinked and realized Vivi and Elijah had smoothed open an old newspaper article across the coffee table.

It faced her, and the headline was all too familiar.

The byline, of course, even more so.

Beverly leaned forward and pressed her hands at the edges, rereading one of her very first stories.

"Temperance," Beverly murmured. "Temperance Temper." She crinkled her eyebrows and glanced up. "Such an odd name, huh?"

"Lots of those flying around here," Elijah pointed out.

"True. I remember this story. I even went to Detroit to interview the family. I got to stay in a Best Western for the trip. One night only. Two meals. Expensed. Now if we travel, it's on our own dime." She laughed. "Funny how budgets ebb and flow in small towns."

"Was Kayla born yet?" Elijah asked. "It was written the year we were born." He pointed to the date.

"No. I—no. She wasn't." Beverly didn't add that she got pregnant right after the story released. They had a party, there in their new house on Apple Hill. Tom invited school people. Beverly invited the paper. The tipsy couple snuck into their bedroom smack-dab in the middle of the party. There was a point at which Tom joked they should name the baby Temperance, if it was a girl. At the time, Beverly thought it was a hilarious joke. Not even morbid. Not back then, when the idea of this Temperance woman was exciting. And even now, the thought of the woman stimulated that old reporterly feeling. The hope persisted. She'd be old, sure, but she *could* be alive.

In the end, Beverly wrote off Tom's joke as just that. He'd gotten irritable, insisting Temperance was a perfect name for their daughter. Beverly disagreed. At that, he'd tried for something literary. Daisy or Elizabeth or even Hester or Matilda.

Beverly liked Kayla, though. It had more depth than Tom believed. He figured it was a trendy name, and maybe it had become that. But Kayla was Beverly's name. It was the name she'd set in high school— back when she'd dreamed about her wedding day and last name and baby names. It was always Kayla. Kayla and Dylan. Out popped a girl, so logically, it had to be Kayla.

Maybe she was a Daisy or Elizabeth or even Hester or Matilda...

Beverly shook the thought. Kayla didn't die because of her name.

"So, what happened?" Vivi asked, pulling Beverly back to the present.

"With Temperance?" Beverly sighed. "It was a dead end. I did two more stories, follow-up pieces, but—"

"Yeah," Elijah interrupted with a sigh of his own. "We found those, too."

"You found those where you found this one? At your house?" Beverly directed the inquiry at Vivi.

"No," Vivi answered. "The other articles we found online. It was only this one we found in Carl's stack."

"Stack?"

"Of newspapers. He had stacks of them."

Beverly slotted away this knowledge. He was either a record keeper or a hoarder. Likely *both*.

She turned her reporter persona on. "How did you discover this one? Were you going through each newspaper edition?"

Vivi shook her head. "It was sitting right on top. We made it about ten more papers down until we figured we could look online."

"I had to pay for access, though." Elijah said this like it was a point of pride. Like he had provided something for Vivi.

Beverly suppressed a knowing grin. "Nice." Then, she shook her head. "But, again, nothing came up. The local family ended up accepting that she'd run away. That was it."

"Does she still have family here?"

Frowning, Beverly answered, "I don't think so. They probably all moved or passed. My mom would know. Why are you two looking into this?"

"Well," Vivi began, "my history teacher gave us an assignment to study local history. We had to come up with a thesis statement, and a thesis statement has to have a twinge of controversy, he says."

"Mr. Castle said the same thing," Elijah added.

"Oh, right." Beverly pursed her lips. There was plenty of old-time controversy in town. All these two had to do was turn over a couple of stones. Dig around. They'd find it, all right. She nodded. "My mom is the person you should speak with. Bertie Gillespie. I'll give you her number, but you can swing by the B&B anytime you'd like."

"That's *perfect*." Vivi stood and reached for the newspaper, and her hand knocked Beverly's stack of papers out of place. As Beverly moved to straighten them, Sandy rose, too, whapping her tail against the coffee table. The pages fluttered out of order, and a single pink sheet caught on the draft and sailed over Sandy's back onto the floor.

"Whoops." Elijah plucked it and passed it over to Beverly.

"Thanks again," Vivi gushed. "We'll just go over there now. To the B&B, I mean."

Beverly took the page and nodded, walking them to the door, which she closed and locked.

Back in the living room, she glanced down at the limp paper. It was a carbon copy of something else—the long-dried ink having faded on the original, too, no doubt.

An ache settling in the base of her skull, Beverly knew she needed coffee *stat*.

It was time to get ready for the day—or at least, for the evening with Darry.

She headed to the kitchen to start a fresh pot of the good stuff, but first, she lay the pink paper on top of the stack, saving it to review later. *After* her date.

CHAPTER 28—BEVERLY

I t wasn't a date, *per se*. It was a meeting.

But neither one had dressed for a meeting.

Darry had picked her up in a spit-clean, mint-condition, white-with-black-trim BMW. When she complimented it, he told her it was little more than a relic, really. "A '94. My dad's," he'd said, his hands deep in his pockets as they strode awkwardly from her front door to the Beemer.

He wore a red-and-black flannel shirt, the sleeves pushed up to his elbows revealing sinewy, tanned forearms. Form-fitting jeans concealed brown boots. His hair was gelled, and he smelled like cloves. He was all local. Nothing like his principal persona. Nothing, either, like Tom.

She wore black leggings and a dusty pink blouse

—billowy and soft. Her trusty blue bracelet and a pair of authentic diamond stud earrings that she had given Kayla for her eighth grade promotion. Sometimes it felt odd wearing Kayla's things, like Beverly was stealing. Sometimes, though, it felt right. Like her daughter was close to her.

Tonight, it felt right.

They arrived at Eat Street with a rush of other Saturday night diners, but the waitress was a friend of Kayla's—go figure—and she waved Beverly and Darry through the crowd at the hostess stand.

Beverly didn't like this sort of preferential treatment, and especially not when she was with, well, a man who wasn't Tom. Even after his death. Maybe *especially* after his death.

She let it go, though, in favor of scavenging for some pebble of truth in a pile of pain.

"I can bring water or soft drinks. Not the hard stuff, though. You'll have to wait for the real server," the girl said. It was innocent enough. Presumptuous, but innocent. Still, Beverly felt herself get warm in the neck. Splotchy, probably.

She made light. "Oh, hah. Just a water for me."

"I'll take a hot cocoa," Darry replied with a warm smile.

Knitting her eyebrows anxiously, Beverly flattened her hand on the table in front of the well-meaning girl. "Make that two."

"How was your day?" Darry began, his palms open, expression soft.

She fell back decades. To another time they'd been here, at Eat Street. In all, not much had changed. And, well, everything had changed.

Beverly tried to pretend that she could see Darry as the grown-up professional he was. "Weird, actually. The neighbor kids—you know Elijah? Elijah Best."

He nodded.

"He and Vivi, the new girl." She lowered her chin. "You know Vivi?"

"Nice girl," he replied. "Different."

"Different?" Beverly felt reporter mode kicking in, but she tamped it down. "She's a beautiful girl."

"Ethereally so," Darry agreed. "But that isn't what stands out."

Beverly was caught off guard by this. "Really?" Vivi was stunning. So stunning that she was almost odd-looking. Like an out-of-place supermodel in a teenager's body.

"She spends all her time with Elijah. Even made a special request to have her schedule rearranged." He shook his head. "We couldn't oblige, but she's...at once both confident and scared as a mouse."

"Hm." Beverly stowed the nugget away. "Anyway, they came by digging up history. This old article—actually, this old *series* I wrote about some woman who went missing. I guess they've decided to take it on as their history research assignment."

Darry nodded. "Right. Belinger's class. 'Local Lore and Small-Town Secrets.'" He chuckled. "It's caused problems before."

Beverly's ears perked up. "Problems?" she asked. "Like...Belinger's gotten in trouble for the assignment?"

Darry cocked his head and scratched his neck. "No?" Then, he lowered his voice. "Look, Bev, I can't do this. I can't tell you if I wrote up Christie Spectre. I can't even tell you if I ever wrote up Tom. It could mean my *job*, Bev."

"I'm not asking you to give up those details," she protested, a sly smile curling her lips. "Actually, my biggest question is very simple."

He appeared to relax. The waitress dropped off two mugs, each topped with an absurdly towering mound of whipped cream.

"What can I get you two?" the waitress asked. A different girl. A tad older. Just as familiar.

Darry held his hand in gesture for Beverly to order. She asked for the number four.

Darry copied her order.

The waitress left, and Beverly leaned forward.

"You said Tom didn't run the creative writing club. If he didn't, then who did?"

He gave her a hard look. Seconds passed. The noise in the diner grew to a pinnacle then ebbed low to a valley. Forks and knives clattered on plates. Laughter sputtered to life and tuckered out.

Darry folded his arms and inched closer. "Bev, you *know* who ran the club."

The look in his eyes was half sadness, half something else. Not pity, no. A dare?

She nodded carefully. "Did you like her?" She hadn't planned to ask that. It just fell out.

But gone were the stilted delays. The moments to measure words and consider audience. They'd found a rhythm. In the noise of Eat Street on Main in the little Michigan town where they had shared their first kiss.

"She was a snake. If it wasn't one thing that meant her undoing, it was sure to be another. You didn't hear that from me, but Bev"—he frowned —"you knew all along. Didn't you?"

Shaking her head, Beverly caught the waitress

heading their way. Two matching plates balanced on one of her arms—the French dip and curly fries. One of Eat Street's best-loved comfort meals.

After thanking the girl and settling into their first bites, Beverly answered Darry. "We had Kayla. We had...*love*." Despite their past, Beverly found it easy to share all of this with Darry.

"I get it." He took a hearty bite of his sandwich and spoke with a full mouth. Some things never changed. "I loved Monica. Thought I did."

"Love changes, you know." Beverly took her own bite, not bothering to dab her lips anxiously, like she might if this were a first date with a handsome stranger. Indeed, it might be a date. And Darry was handsome. But neither was a stranger to the other.

"I disagree." Darry's gaze froze on her. His hands were pressed to the table, on either side of his plate. His Adam's apple bobbed.

"You don't think love can change?"

"I think people can change. I think people do things to change their love. How they love. *If* they love. But...*real* true love"—he shook his head —"doesn't change."

Beverly's pulse quickened. She lowered her food back to its plate, dropping it. Her appetite vanished, and her stomach churned.

In that moment, she missed Kayla more than ever. Kayla would have something to say about real true love. Real true love was that between girl-friends. Sisters. Real true love was that between mother and daughter.

Nausea churned in Beverly's stomach. She tried to swallow it down with the lump in her throat, but tears broke out along her lash line. Her sinuses cleared like the calm before a storm, and her mind went wild. She shouldn't be there, at Eat Street. She shouldn't be living her life, eating dinner with old friends—old flames. She shouldn't be smiling or happy or *living*. Everyone and everything should be dead along with Tom and Kayla and Beverly's only-ever known happiness. Including real true love. It was dead, too. Six feet under.

"Love can die," she managed, her voice hoarse as a single tear burst over the levy of her eyelid.

"People die," Darry murmured back, his hand finding its way to hers where she gripped the edge of the table. He didn't squeeze it or rub, he just rested it there while he locked eyes with her. "People die, Beverly. Love doesn't."

Stumbling, climbing through the thick haze of grief, his words seized Beverly. Real true love didn't die. It didn't even die if the one you loved died.

Kayla had been the love of Beverly's life. Plainly. And she'd never have to explain that to anyone. Not Darry, not anyone.

Could there be something else now that Kayla was gone? Could there be a different love to grow in the desert of Beverly's heart?

Maybe Darry was right, though. Maybe there already was a little love left in there. Maybe nothing new had to grow at all. Maybe the seed had been dormant since high school. And now? Now she had the chance to water it.

CHAPTER 29—BEVERLY

After finishing their meal in a throbbing sort of silence, Darry drove Beverly home.

Once there, in the moonlit, porch-lit dimness, they sat for a long moment. She'd left her porch light on—or rather, she'd never again turned it off after the crash. She didn't turn off most of her lights, in fact. Preferring the comfort of the hum of electricity. Proof of life beyond her own.

Soon, though, the bulb would die. A miracle it hadn't yet. Maybe God—or whoever was up there—had gifted Beverly this one grace.

The light of that hanging lamp cast its glow across her front door, bringing out the blue.

She swallowed hard. "Kayla and I both love blue.

Tom didn't, though." She laughed. "He forbade I do anything 'wild' like paint the front door. He was more of a natural wood type."

"Not one to draw attention?" Even as Darry said it, her stomach twisted.

Scoffing, Beverly answered, "I guess that was the goal."

"I didn't mean to imply—"

She spun toward Darry, eyeing him in the darkened cab. "It makes it easier in some ways, though. You know?"

"What makes what easier?" His voice was soft, the question lame, and Beverly didn't much feel like explaining.

Sighing, she said, "Never mind."

But Darry's hand found hers, covering it along the exposed side of her seat. "No. Tell me. If you want to, I mean."

Beverly chewed the insides of her cheeks but managed a reply. "Hating Tom." She glanced at Darry. "Hating Tom makes it a little easier."

"I get that." He stared ahead then dropped his voice low for his next comment. "As long as you don't hate yourself, too."

She withdrew her hand from beneath his. "Of course I hate myself." It came out on a laugh. Like, *duh*, she hated herself. What mother wouldn't be filled with self-loathing when her daughter did the one thing that moms were supposed to warn against? Beat out of their children? Somewhere, somehow, Beverly had failed Kayla. Maybe Tom did, too, but he wasn't around to share the blame. So it was just Beverly. All Beverly.

Darry unbuckled his seat belt and moved to open the door.

"No—" she started.

"I was going to open your door is all."

"Just—*sit* with me a minute." She reached for his hand and squeezed it. Maybe she could lose herself tonight. Maybe that would be the impetus for true healing. Doing something so destructive that she could be the villain she figured she'd become on that fateful day the year before.

Darry stilled, allowing her to crush his fingers together. Then, he spoke again. "I can't imagine what you've been through, Bev."

Shaking her head, she scoffed. "I can hardly imagine it myself."

Her eyes turned twitchy. She glanced at the clock in the dash. She should call it a night. Get some real sleep. Start fresh tomorrow, on the Carlson case. Tell Forrest it was over. She'd let everything go. Everything about the school and about Tom and Christie.

What good would it do to antagonize the school? To paint them as the bad guy? It'd hurt Darry. And it'd get her nowhere.

No. Beverly wasn't going to be that woman. That woman who pinned her life to tragedy and her heart to bitterness.

Kayla was dead.

And so was her cheating father.

Something itched at the back of Beverly's brain, though. A need still to know the full extent of the story. To show up at Christie's front door and ask, *Why? Why were you texting my daughter?*

Why did Tom let their daughter text while driving? He was right there in the car with her. In the passenger seat. Beverly had all the brutal details. The phone with that final, innocent text—*Be there soon!*—had wedged perfectly in the base of the crumpled windshield. The recipient got the text. Hadn't replied. Later, they learned that the Spectres had invited Tom and Kayla so that Mr. Spectre could work with Kayla on piano. She'd always wanted to learn.

Beverly had the sudden need to get out of Darry's car. The sudden delayed trauma about cars altogether. Maybe she'd start riding a bike. Or walking. Or taking the bus.

She unstrapped herself and pushed the door open.

"I'll walk you to your door." Darry rushed out and around like she might fall.

But it was too late for that. Beverly had already fallen. A long time ago.

CHAPTER 30—BEVERLY

They reached her front door, and Beverly found herself pressing her palms to Darry's chest, leaning into him as her energy dissipated into the crisp, autumn night air.

"I don't say this for any reason other than true concern," Darry started, holding Beverly against him in a sterile hug. "I don't know if you should be alone." He was quick to add, "I could call a friend for you? Maybe Jude—she's next door, right? We could go there or she could come here?"

Beverly pushed back and stared up at him. "You're my friend, right?"

He licked his lips and nodded. "Beverly, I—"

She regained some strength and retrieved her key from her purse, pushed it perfunctorily into the doorknob and then the dead bolt, turning the gears and opening the quiet, empty house with the lights still on. "It'll be like old times," Beverly said, waiting for him just inside the threshold.

"How do you mean?" He stood there looking every bit the awkward teenage boy he'd been those many years ago.

"My sneaking you into my house." Except now it wasn't just *her* house. Kayla's presence hung around. Tom's, too.

Did Kayla like her principal? Beverly had a sudden need to know. She let the question come out. "Did Kayla like you?"

He remained on the porch and scratched the back of his head. "Did Kayla like me? I mean—I don't know. I think so? She was a great kid, Bev. Only interaction I had was doling out awards to her at the quarterly assembly in October."

"She won awards?"

"Sure." He blinked. "Perfect attendance. Principal's List, too."

Beverly nodded. "Right. I knew about those." She peered at him again. "And *you* gave them to her?"

He shrugged. "She shook my hand and thanked me. Then sort of ducked away. She was every bit a freshman, socially. Academically, though, Kayla had focus."

Beverly smiled; it felt like a dose of closure. She'd need ten bottles more, but this was a start.

"Darry—" His name curled over her tongue sensually, surprising Beverly. She pushed on. "Want to come in?"

He shook his head. "I really better not—"

"No, I don't mean—I just mean...to sit and talk? I have some cocoa powder somewhere. Or iced tea?"

"Just until you're comfortable?" Though he asked as tentatively as a mouse, he also stepped over the threshold.

Another dose.

Beverly's chest clenched and loosened and clenched again. Her house wasn't a mess, no, but she hadn't expected company. Now that Darry Ruthenberg was inside, she saw the foyer differently. Unopened mail overfilling the silver plate at the table. Galoshes peeking out from beneath the bench. Beyond, in the parlor, a blanket thrown haphazardly over the back of the sofa—and not in a way that looked hip and fashionable, but in a way that looked sloppy. "Here, let's, um..." She glanced through to the kitchen. Dishes piled in the sink. "Let's just sit in here." She gestured to the room where she'd hosted Elijah and Vivi earlier that day, quickly folding the blanket in a neat pleat and resting it gracefully across one arm. Then, Beverly lowered to the sofa.

Darry hovered by the armchair, but she scooted over and patted the cushion next to her.

"Oh, right. Can I get you a drink?"

"Sure," he said, more brightly now. "Whatever you're having."

She pushed back up off the sofa, nervous and jittery now. "I'll, um, be right back." She backed into the coffee table accidentally, and the stack of old papers from Jude's classroom closet spilled onto the rug in between the table and the sofa.

"Dammit," Beverly muttered, bending to collect them.

"I got it," Darry offered, kneeling down and pulling the pages back together.

She faltered over whether to *let* him. Would he recognize them? Would he immediately know they were remnants from his own school building?"

Beverly grabbed the sheet in his hands and fumbled beneath the coffee table for as many more as she could reach, hastily compiling them and then carrying them with her into the kitchen. "Got it, thanks!"

In the kitchen, she put on a fresh pot of coffee. It'd keep her up, sure, but it was the only thing that tempted her away from opening a bottle of wine from atop the fridge.

She returned to the parlor to inform Darry of the brewing beverage, but as she stepped through the doorway, she saw that he held a pink slip of paper in his hands.

His jaw was set and its tendons worked visibly as he studied it.

"What's that?" Beverly knew it was the pink page that had floated about earlier. She hadn't looked at it yet, assuming it was something disciplinary. She laughed anxiously, but it came out high and tight. "A detention slip? Not for Kayla, though..." Or was it?

Darry looked up. "Not for Kayla, no." He examined the page again. "Where did you find this?"

Beverly stammered. "I, um...it was..."

"Did *Tom* have it?"

The question threw her for a loop. Her eyebrows shot up her forehead. "Tom? Why *would* he?" She all but dashed the short way to the sofa and leaned over its back to read over Darry's shoulder.

The header on the blush-colored page arrested her.

.   .   .

NOTICE OF TERMINATION *of Contract between Harbor Hills Unified School District #4 and Mrs. Christie Spectre.*

HER EYES FLEW BACK UP to the sender and addressee.

HARBOR HILLS UNIFIED *School District*
  1200 Schoolhouse Street
  Harbor Hills, Michigan
  (555) 297-1699

MRS. CHRISTIE SPECTRE
  PO Box 2233
  Pinconning, Michigan
  (555) 456-5426

BEVERLY SWIPED a strand of hair from her eyes and leaned lower over Darry's shoulder. He held the page perfectly still.

.   .   .

THIS NOTICE CONCERNS the termination of Mrs. Christie Spectre's continuing teaching contract. The cause of discontinuation is unprofessional conduct. The above employee was found to be noncompliant with regards to Faculty Policy 3b: Intra-faculty fraternization.

DETAILS of the prior investigation into this conduct and termination of this contract can be found in district records at 1200 Schoolhouse Street, Harbor Hills, Michigan.

MRS. SPECTRE, Harbor Hills wishes you the best.

RESPECTFULLY,
    Dr. Jeffrey Shendz
    Superintendent of Harbor Hills Unified School District

"IT WAS IN JUDE'S STUFF," Beverly confessed. She had a sick feeling in her stomach as she backed slowly away from the sofa.

Darry stood and lowered the page. "What do you

mean? Did Jude drop a box of...*recycling* over here or something?"

God bless him, he was trying to give her an out. And Jude one, too.

Beverly weighed her choices. She could nod her head, but then what if it came up again? What if Jude mentioned something? The matter could get messy. The last thing Beverly wanted was for either Jude or Darry to get in trouble.

But then, she was pretty darn curious about all this. Christie was *fired*? Was Tom set to be fired, too?

Questions erupted in Beverly's brain, but she still had to answer Darry's question.

"Jude invited me to her classroom for lunch. I stole a file. I took it, I mean. Jude didn't give it to me. I *had* to know. For *sure*, Darry. About Tom and Christie."

"How would it change anything, Bev?"

She swallowed hard, her gut cramping. It could change everything. It could make Tom complicit, even more than he already was. It could relieve Beverly of the brunt of the burden—of the guilt. But she couldn't explain all that to Darry.

Not unless there really could be more to the story. More that she didn't know. That could somehow save her sanity. So, she shrugged. "Grief makes you do crazy things?" She meant it lightly, as a joke, but it came out morbid and crass.

To her surprise, though, he cracked a smile. "You already have the answer on this, Bev." He gestured to the pink paper. "I was effectively precluded from the decision. It was a no-brainer, anyway." He pushed his hand through his hair and bent down, leaving the page on the coffee table. Not folding it and tucking it into his pocket. Not tearing it to shreds or shaking it at Beverly like an angry father.

He left it for her. To do with what she would.

"I won't pretend to know what will help you move on." He pushed air through his lips. "Hell, maybe there is no moving on from a tragedy like that. I guess it's impossible."

"I'll never move on from Kayla's death," Beverly replied. Her shoulders relaxed. She could hear that the coffee had finished percolating. Darry grew at ease once again, settling back onto the sofa like he might stay for a spell.

Beverly turned to get their coffee but stopped and took a gulp of air. "As for Tom? Let's just say I'd already started to move on...when he was *alive*."

CHAPTER 31—ANNETTE

Late September in Harbor Hills was a knot of confusion, so far as the weather was concerned. God kept folks on their toes with increasingly cool nights and still-warm days. Hot, in fact.

But the last Saturday of September, the weather was just right for another yard sale.

This time, Annette's. Over the past few weeks, they'd made great progress on packing and configuring things with Tad and Elora.

But Elijah and Vivi *still* hadn't finished the fort, and they planned to be out of there on October 1. The goal was to stay well ahead of Elora's due date, and naturally this put a supreme amount of pressure on everyone.

Instead of helping Annette and Roman, they'd thrown everything into their partner research project: the ridiculous hunt for Temperance Temper. Their paper was due the following Monday, and this complicated everything.

That morning, all the ladies of the street were set to join Annette and Roman at their sale. It wasn't as sweeping as Quinn's had been. After all, they were only downsizing by degrees, not cleaning a hoard. Annette was nothing if not neat.

Quinn and Vivi appeared first, but Vivi just as soon disappeared upstairs in search of Elijah.

"When's the wedding?" Quinn joked, passing two boxes of doughnuts to Annette.

"No kidding. I've never seen him find his *person* like this. Even his guy friends have sort of just fallen by the wayside. It's...interesting." Annette didn't share that she got a little thrill of Vivi being Elijah's first maybe-girlfriend. But it wasn't something they could talk about freely, especially in Beverly's presence.

"Coffee?" Annette offered a to-go mug. She'd stationed them in a row, ready to grab and go.

Quinn first extracted a doughnut then scooped up a coffee and they walked together toward the garage. Originally, the house had only a barn.

Roman had had it converted to a garage like the other houses on the street had done.

Annette took a shot at digging around a little as she popped the garage light on—blinding them both. "How's work going? With Beverly and Forrest? Are things smooth for you? Are they treating you well? What are your hours like? You seem to come and go some days."

"Oh, it's going well enough. I like it, in fact. Sort of a quiet job. Not many people around the office. Beverly's been doing her story on the school district. I think she interviewed Darry, the principal. Last weekend maybe? She sort of fell off the radar after that. Probably busy meeting deadline."

Annette knitted her brows together. "What kind of story is it, exactly? A revenge piece?"

"Revenge?" Quinn looked at her curiously as the garage door groaned to life and yawned open, revealing to the world all the hard work Annette had done to prepare for the day. Organized folding tables with goods categorized by price. Rows of furniture pieces Roman had brought out, stationed by the door—quick and easy access for him to tug onto the driveway.

Annette didn't bother to glance Quinn's way. "Of course. Beverly and Darry *dated* all through high school. They were high school sweethearts, so the rumors go. Destined to marry, and then...*didn't*."

"He ended it?" Quinn asked.

Annette shrugged. "No one knows the full story. I just assumed that if Beverly is slamming the district, it's got to do with that."

"Not with the car crash? Her daughter's death? And husband's?"

Annette scoffed. "What would the school have to do with that?" They were walking down the drive now, each lifting one end of the small cashbox table —the same one Annette had loaned to Quinn for her yard sale.

Quinn gave her a bemused look. "Vivi says there are rumors swirling."

Annette nearly dropped the table when someone spoke behind her. "Rumors of what?" Jude and Beverly had walked up together.

Everyone froze. Stares of ice all around.

Quinn put all her focus on situating the table so that it was perfectly square to the corner of the drive. She blinked then looked up, settling her gaze firmly on Beverly. "Rumors that Tom was cheating on you."

CHAPTER 32—QUINN

Quinn's breath hitched in her chest. She didn't know Beverly well, and of course she'd never met Tom. Was the affair...*recent*? Was it with someone Quinn had met? In *town*? Had she come across this woman in her social media interactions for the paper? Maybe the affair partner was a woman who'd commented her disgust with the new town council election results. Or perhaps she was the oddball who kept posting her junk for sale on the page— something that Quinn had to delete every time.

After a painful several moments, Quinn cleared her throat. "I'm sorry." She gave Beverly an earnest look. "I should keep my mouth shut."

But to everyone's surprise Beverly's hardness

broke, and she batted a hand. "Yeah. It's pretty clear that something was going on between him and Christie Spectre." Then, as if she were simply recanting a story about a couple of other locals, Beverly added, "She used to live across town. Taught at the high school with Tom. Her husband was going to teach Kayla piano, too. Apparently."

Annette spoke up. "She was the worst teacher that school ever had. Probably got fired. Pfft."

"Actually," Beverly answered, a wry grin growing across her face, "she was. But not because of her bum teaching skills."

Jude turned and narrowed her eyes on Beverly. "You went through my things?"

Beverly nodded. "It was in a folder from your office. A pink slip. Indecent conduct. *Fraternization.*"

"A folder from my office?" Jude scrunched her face.

"Yes?" Beverly answered in a question.

Jude turned pale. "I—I didn't know there was other evidence." She glanced around. "I found a pink slip, too. I kept it from you, because—"

"Why?" Beverly asked.

"I know what it's like to have other people stir up trouble in your life. I didn't want to do that."

Beverly shook her head. "You didn't. Tom and Christie did."

"I'm so sorry, Beverly," Quinn murmured.

Again, though, Beverly waved her off. "I'm not. It's over. All of it." She lifted her chin.

"But you're writing a piece for the paper—" Quinn began, instantly regretting the dumb comment.

Beverly sighed loudly. "I might not. I might go back to the Carlson story." She jerked her chin up toward Quinn's house. "Seems like I have some accomplices to help, anyway."

"Why *were* you writing about the school, anyway?" Annette asked. "Was it to throw that dashing old principal under the bus?" Then she rolled her eyes over to Quinn. "If Roman ever cheated on me, I'd probably have it out for every man that ever broke my heart, too."

"Darry didn't break my heart. We were just kids when we went out."

Jude jumped to reply. Quinn saw a flicker in her eyes. "Darry Ruthenberg? The principal? I didn't —*realize*. Is Annette right? Is that why you were writing a piece on the school?"

Beverly shook her head adamantly. "No. No, no. I was writing a piece...because..." A sigh lifted her chest, and she stared off, blinking and thinking for a beat. "I just can't believe Kayla was texting and driving. I don't *want* to believe it. Because if she *was*, then it's my fault, you know?" Beverly's voice trembled, and Quinn's heart ached hard for the poor woman.

"It wasn't your fault. And anyway," Annette asserted, "how can you even be sure she was texting and driving?"

"Her phone," Beverly shot back, almost defensive in an ironic and tragic way. "There was a text. They were heading to Christie's house. For piano lessons." The sentences came out choppy, and Quinn could see that Beverly was on the verge of breaking down.

"You should write the Carlson story. You can come raid my house and the garage. You'll find lots of gems, I bet. The kids can help. It'll be a smash hit. It'll propel the *Herald* into journalism history." Quinn gave her a winning look, and Beverly returned a soft smile.

"That's what I'm thinking," Beverly answered.

But Jude was quick to step in, brimming with fervor. "Why not do a write-up on Tom? Who says the dead are protected from the truth?"

Annette snorted. "Whoever coined the idea that the living shouldn't speak ill of the dead?"

Silence spilled over them. A late-season bird chirped from a high-up spot in an oak tree. The sun burned one degree skyward. Quinn shivered in the early-morning air.

Laughter bubbled from Annette's house. The kids. Unaware of the somber conversation cracking open on the driveway.

Finally, Jude spoke. "We give these men a pass. The rotten ones, I mean. I gave Gene that pass for years. Until it came out that he was even more than a playboy. Even *worse*. Way worse, it turned out."

"See," Annette replied, "you can only say that because he's still alive. Maybe Gene isn't here to defend himself, but he's not dead."

"Yet," Jude grunted.

Quinn laughed in spite of herself, and Jude turned an icy stare on her.

"Quinn, you probably have plenty ill to speak of Vivi's dad, right?"

But Quinn frowned. "I mean...our marriage was crap. But Matt's a good guy. Just a bad fit."

"Did he cheat?" Beverly asked.

"No." Quinn's answer came easily. "But in the end, there was someone else. Long after Matt and I parted ways." She looked thoughtful. "I'd like to think there's someone else for me, too. I think that's sort of my driving hope. Especially now that Vivi is older. She'll be gone soon, you know?" She didn't share the crush she'd developed lately, but even so Annette read it on her face.

"Oh, my gosh. Those Jericho men. I *swear*." Annette laughed gleefully.

"What do you mean *those Jericho men*?" Jude asked, lightening up. "As in...Dean? You know he'll be working on my house. Is there something I should know?"

"Just that they're lady-killers." She wiggled her brows at Quinn. "Twenty bucks and a mimosa say Quinn's got it for Forrest."

"Ew," Beverly answered. "You're talking about my cousins."

"Your handsome cousins," Annette shot back.

Beverly rolled her eyes. "Anyway, Tom's affair is old news. The only reason I was chasing it down was to"—she took in a long breath—"get closure. Or maybe free myself from guilt, you know? If Tom was the bad guy, then I was less the bad mom. Some-how." She blinked and shook her head.

"You were an exceptional mother, Beverly," Annette answered quietly. "Everyone knows that. Kayla made good decisions. What happened was an *accident*. You cannot blame yourself."

Quinn worked her jaw, wondering whether to interject her own anecdote and thoughts here. Like, for example, the truth that you could only control your child's choices so much. Still, Quinn knew the pain of self-blame. When Vivi ran away, she cursed herself for not being easier to talk to. Kinder. More patient. And then also more of a disciplinarian. Maybe Vivi wouldn't be so strong-willed if Quinn and Matt were firmer with her. There was never a clear path to good parenting. Not in Quinn's addled brain, at least. She kept quiet.

"Why don't you write a different article entirely?" Quinn suggested.

Beverly asked, "What do you mean? And skip the Carlson piece?"

"You need to write about Tom. Or at least do a story about how husbands fail their wives." Jude's words were acid but her tone was deflated. "Sorry," she muttered. "I'm just—still hurt. I can relate to your pain, Beverly. About Tom."

"Save the Carlson piece for later," Quinn said. "Do a story about...being a woman. A wife. A mother. A widow. A—"

"What's the opposite of orphan? Because I'm mostly that," Beverly said with a sad smile, but her eyes crinkled and her posture relaxed. She was okay, Quinn thought. Beverly was okay.

"Who knows?" Jude answered. "But you're still Kayla's mother." Her affect had shifted, too. She'd closed the gap around the table, her arms no longer folded defensively but now hanging in front of her waist, her nails picking at themselves.

"And you're a neighbor, don't forget," Annette added.

"And a dog owner," Jude pointed out. They were on a roll.

"And a journalist," Quinn added. "Who loves the color blue. From what I can tell."

"That's right!" Annette cried. "You're the woman who lives in the house with the blue front door."

"And you're a respected community member," Quinn said. "People look to your articles for the latest news around town, right? People talk about Beverly Castle, who breaks the news."

Annette smirked. "Yeah, but she usually writes juicy dramatic pieces. That's why the Carlson piece is *perfect*."

"Carlson can wait. You know what you need, Beverly?" Quinn asked.

"What?"

"You need a way to write through your feelings. A channel or an avenue."

Jude lifted a finger. "You know what this town needs?"

Quinn braced herself for another attack of man-hatred.

It didn't come.

Jude's eyes twinkled in the early-morning sun. "This town needs its very own Dear Abby."

CHAPTER 33—JUDE

The yard sale was supposed to begin at eight, which was why Annette didn't send Vivi and Elijah around with the signs until 7:45 a.m. But small-town yard-salers are buzzards, looping around the usual hotspots, and within ten minutes of the kids' departure, a slow trickle of cars emerged on Apple Hill.

By the time flannel-shirted men and cash-clutching ladies made their way from the cars to come assess the offerings, the women of Apple Hill were forced to shut down their brainstorm.

Jude was excited for Beverly. Mainly because she'd found a way to focus her feelings. Dealing with trauma was a tricky thing. Writing seemed to be

Beverly's mainstay, and though Jude agreed that there was little sense in taking down the high school, coming up with an advice column could be a great idea. Until Beverly found her way back to Carl Carlson.

Still, though, Jude would fight for Beverly. The time to cover Carlson was far off. First, the poor woman needed to take care of her heart. And Jude knew all too well that distractions could take a grief-stricken mourner only *so* far.

Jude herself could only pitch in at the yard sale for so long. At nine, Dean Jericho was due to start work on the pony wall. Demo and cleanup.

By 8:30, Jude figured she'd better head home to freshen herself up. She glanced around for Annette, to bid her good luck. Roman had appeared and was huddled near Tad and Elora, the couple who'd be buying the Best house. Jude might say she'd miss being so near to Annette, but then they'd still technically be neighbors...only instead of down the street from one another, they'd be around the corner.

She hadn't gotten to know Roman very well.

Annette stood, hands on hips, talking with Vivi and Elijah. Maybe giving them something else to do. Vivi then pointed as if over the Best house, and

Annette nodded. The two teenagers took off toward the backyard gate, on a new mission. Jude hoped they had enough to distract them away from that oddball Carl Carlson. It was unbecoming for kids to get too caught up in the macabre, and Jude considered the Carlson matter to be just that: unsuitable.

"Jude!"

She whipped around. "Oh, Beverly." Jude bit her lower lip. "About the Dear Abby idea, I don't want to tell you what to write…"

"I think it's a great suggestion." This came from Quinn, who wore a fanny pack that she kept zipping and unzipping compulsively. Her eyes twitched into a fit of blinking. "Everybody loves telling other people what to do with their lives," she added.

Jude's heart ached a bit for Quinn. Despite her newly stabilized life, there was a bit of a longing there. Something missing. "Quinn's right, I must say."

"I agree," Beverly answered. "I just need to figure out a name for the feature. Dear Beverly feels like a bit of a rip-off."

"Maybe you should reframe it, somehow," Quinn offered. "Think about it in terms of how women seek comfort and advice, you know?"

"They write to Abby," Beverly quipped.

Jude smiled warmly. "I have to go. Dean Jericho's coming over to start on our project, and I want to make sure everything is *ready*." She didn't mean to overemphasize the word, but it served to bring attention.

"Ohh, yes. Forrest's older, blue-collar brother," Quinn replied.

"Remember, I'm related to them, so I'd appreciate a measure of decency if you two flirts can muster it." Beverly pursed her lips.

At this, Jude laughed hard. Never in her life had anyone called her a flirt. And for good reason. Jude wasn't interested in men. Not anymore. With Gene's exit, she'd found it simpler to kiss goodbye those little extras in life. Flirtations. Affairs. Anything cheery. Now was a point in Jude's life where she was in neutral mode, figuring out who she was. Where she was going. All that.

"I assure you that the only thoughts I have about Dean Jericho are decent ones. He's an electrician. A handyman."

Quinn raised an eyebrow.

Jude felt herself flush. She bristled. "He's coming over to help with the house. That's *it*. I need the little entryway wall gone. Paneling pulled. Some paint. Nothing untoward, I can promise you."

But as she left and made her way to the unadorned two-story with a Maine coon sitting in the window, Jude began to wonder if she'd just made a promise that she might not keep...

CHAPTER 34—BEVERLY

After Jude left to see to her male caller, Beverly turned to Quinn. "What will Forrest think?"

Quinn made a funny face. "About what?"

"About Dear Beverly?"

"Look, Bev. I'm not a marketing genius, but I agree that you need a better column name. Something that's more Harbor Hills. Something all your own. That sets you apart." Quinn fiddled with the zipper on her fanny pack and blinked repeatedly over Beverly's shoulder.

Beverly turned to follow her anxious gaze.

Her heart jumped in her chest, and her breath caught somewhere between her lungs and the back of her throat, finally wheezing out in a weird noise.

"What are you doing here?" she asked Darry as he strode across the street, his hands tucked into his pockets.

He gave her a winning smile, and Quinn floated off. Beverly's stomach flipped and flopped. The last she'd seen of Darry, they'd ended things on an ambiguous note. She'd mentioned that she'd already begun moving on from Tom. He'd hinted that he'd never moved on from her. At least, that's how she'd read his comments about real true love.

But then there was the paralyzing circumstances of the Christie Spectre pink slip and all that *that* meant.

In the end, they'd agreed that there was nothing more to do. That Beverly would redirect her focus. That the truth she was desperate to find—that Tom was the problem and not Beverly as a woman or a wife or a mother—was unnecessary. Because in the end, Beverly was never the problem. Darry had her convinced of this by the time he'd hugged her good-night and scruffed the patches of fur behind Sandy's and Danny's ears.

Now, though, something else bobbed in the atmosphere around them.

"When I saw there was a yard sale in Crabtree

Court, I figured I'd drive over. Are you selling any 1950s Art Deco lamps?"

She laughed. "It's not my yard sale."

"I could have sworn there was one here just a couple of weeks ago."

"There was," Beverly acknowledged, jutting her chin toward Quinn's house. "The neighbor lady."

"So when will you have yours?"

"My what?" she answered, growing aware of just how close he stood to her now that they were both at the corner of the drive, his heels sinking into the grass patch by the mailbox. Her calves burning and stomach clenching as she tried to keep her body from jerking with nerves.

"Your yard sale."

She shook her head. "I don't have a lot of time for that."

"But you're here, at the Best house, helping with *this* one."

"Well, I have time for my friends, of course."

"If you need help, I could help you."

"What? Put on a yard sale?" She laughed him off. "I have nothing to get rid of." They both knew this was a fib. She could start with Tom's closet. From there, move on to his work shed. The garage. There was plenty to sell or give away. Plenty of Tom's things. When it came to Kayla's, however, she could do that only in fits and spurts. On whims and after inspirations, like she had with the fairy lights she'd gifted to Vivi.

Darry accepted her answer, though, and didn't push. "I actually came by to give you something."

Her heart froze, and Beverly feared for a moment that she might pass out.

She didn't, though. "What?" she asked, reminding herself to breathe. It was all so uncomfortable. Suffocating. His presence. His sympathy. And now...a gift?

He blinked and shifted his weight, withdrawing something from his pocket.

Her skin grew flushed, and she knew her neck was turning splotchy. What could he possibly have? A piece of jewelry? No. Ridiculous.

It was paper. A white paper. Not pink.

No envelope, of course. The thing was folded down into a thick square.

Darry kept his gaze on the paper as he unfolded it once. Twice. Three times. Four. He smoothed it down the front of his thigh then passed it to her.

"I thought you made a good point the other night."

"Huh?" She was confused and kept her eyes on him, nervous to read what he handed her.

"You said you thought there was more to the story. About the crash. Tom. Christie." His voice dropped. "Kayla."

"Okay?" She felt her discomfort bloom to a breaking point. She could barf. Or run out of oxygen. Her heart might stop. Anything was possible.

"I hope you won't be angry." He cleared his throat and shoved his hands back into his pockets, nodding toward the note. "I contacted Christie Spectre. By email." He took one tentative step back. His face turned pinched. "That's her response. Bev, you were right. There was more to the story."

CHAPTER 35—BEVERLY

Beverly read the printed-out email with fervor.

Christie Spectre had spilled her guts. And then some.

When she finished reading, she read it again. And by then, her friends had huddled behind her. Quinn patted Beverly's shoulder. Annette took Beverly's hand and gave it a squeeze. Call it women's intuition or girlfriends' instinct, but it was as though they saw Darry and Beverly and *knew*.

"What's it say, Bev?" Annette pressed lightly.

She wiped a tear from her cheek with the back of her hand and glanced back at the page, but the words couldn't travel from her brain to her lips.

"May I?" Darry asked.

Beverly nodded, and he explained the email.

"I took the liberty of getting in touch with Christie. Beverly wondered a lot of things about the night of the crash, and she had a feeling Christie knew more and hadn't come forward. So, I emailed her and explained Beverly's lingering questions. What happened was this: Tom urged Kayla to take piano lessons from Mr. Spectre. Kayla, none the wiser, agreed. Though Tom and Christie hadn't gone so far as to consummate their affair—Christie's words—the emotional part of it was in full effect. On the night of the crash, Tom had texted Christie from Kayla's phone as she drove. Kayla let her dad use it, Christie thinks, just to coordinate their drive to her house. Christie says, they'd already discussed using Kayla as a smokescreen for their budding clandestine relationship. Kayla would go there for lessons. Maybe they'd sometimes meet at the school. Maybe they'd use a code. It was early on. They were figuring things out.

"Anyway, the *day* of the crash, Christie and Tom spoke in the teachers' lounge. Tom would text her from Kayla's phone and drive Kayla over there for a lesson. This was generally above board. Just sort of a way to see each other. Not *do* anything. Obviously not with Kayla there, or so Christie says in the email.

Christie says she didn't think about who would drive. Only after the crash did she learn that it was Kayla behind the wheel. By the time the investigation came out, she knew her tenure at the high school was over. Everything was too much by then. They were taking too many chances. What she pieced together later, after moving, was that Kayla hadn't been the one to text her that night.

"Tom had."

A collective gasp sucked the air up from around Beverly. She found her voice at last, forcing herself to say each word clearly and precisely. "Kayla wasn't texting and driving."

Annette squeezed Beverly's hand harder. "It was just icy. The roads were so icy that night, Beverly," she whispered.

The others murmured their agreement.

Beverly nodded. "It was an accident. Kayla didn't do anything wrong. She wanted to drive. You know Kayla." She gave a soft laugh. "Stubborn as me. She probably sweet-talked her dad. He was prone to giving in to sweet talk." As she said this, a softness welled in her chest for the man she'd grown to loathe. The softness wasn't a new sprung love or affection, no. It wasn't happiness, of course. It was, Beverly realized, forgiveness.

Forgiveness for Tom, who probably didn't deserve it.

But most importantly, forgiveness for herself. For *Beverly*. For the blue widow with her blue blouses and blue bracelet who lived all alone on Apple Hill Lane in the house with the blue front door.

CHAPTER 36—QUINN

Hearing the tragic truth served to make Quinn even more anxious. She realized that, for Beverly, this was relatively relieving. Kayla wasn't some renegade teen with a penchant for breaking the rules and following impulse. She was a girl behind a wheel on an icy Michigan road. And her father, even from the grave, could still share the brunt of pain with Beverly. He was still rotten, but not so rotten as to let his daughter text while driving.

Quinn could see that this was the closure that Beverly needed. No, the pain wouldn't disappear. The heartache might even still grow. She'd continue to struggle. To wear blue and to avoid the office in favor of seeking out a story that could tear her mind away from her personal life. But she could stop blaming herself and living in self-loathing.

For Quinn, though, the truth about the driving accident compounded her worries, which had lately crawled back into the fold. That was the thing about being a mother—fears lurked in every nook and cranny of life. They were unending, clamping around her throat like a choke chain on a dog.

The little group of them had thinned out now. Annette had slipped away to collect cash from an ambitious yard-saler. Darry lingered nearby, and Quinn sensed that he wanted a moment alone with Beverly.

She cupped her friend's elbow. "Beverly, I think the newspaper feature is a great idea. It's a good way for you to...*process* things, I think. Short of like seeing a shrink."

Beverly nodded. "I have seen a therapist. It helps. So does medicine. But writing...that's the *real* treatment."

"If you want, I can pitch the idea to Forrest? I'm..." Quinn felt her face flush. She cleared throat. "I was going to see him later. For work stuff."

Beverly raised her eyebrows. "*Work* stuff?"

Shrugging, Quinn backtracked. "I mean, I think if we go the route of pitching this as a way to draw in a younger readership and tap into social media, he'll be excited. Maybe he'll have you switch gears now, while we haven't gotten too far with promotional posts."

Beverly groaned. "Right. *Promotions*. Forrest wanted something 'productive,' right? This is super productive. I mean, does it really have to be tied to the school? Why does he care so much about teacher turnover, anyway? Especially if it's not the Tom-and-Christie drama he's after?"

Quinn chewed her lower lip. In fact, she knew *exactly* why Forrest was interested in the behind-the-scenes at Hills High. But she also knew better than to share. Not yet, at least. Not until she wasn't the only keeper of that particular secret.

She swallowed it down. "Like I said. Let's get the ball rolling now. Today. Stay ahead of it all."

"I don't have a direction yet," Beverly answered. "Not *really*. I mean, Dear Beverly is great in theory, but who am I to give life advice? What person would take tips from a widow with the blues?"

"Maybe it's not an advice column. Maybe it's—" Quinn glanced up and around, her fingers tapping out secret words on the pads of her thumbs. An idea struck her. "Maybe it's like a Page 6 sort of thing—a gossip column. Or...you know that show *Bridgerton*? They have a little gossip rag circulating. Something like that." Quinn stopped tapping her fingers and started blinking. It was a fabulous idea.

"Oh, my gosh, *yeah*. Like an anonymous social commentary." Beverly's eyes were wide, but her mouth fell into a frown. "It can't be anonymous, though. Not *really*. It has to be my piece. My byline."

"Then don't have it be totally anonymous. Make it a little lighter. Not strictly *gossip*. Just...fun. Observations from Apple Hill Lane."

"That's cute," Beverly agreed, but Quinn could see her mind was spinning. "Or, how about A View of Harbor Hills."

"Also adorable," Quinn confirmed.

Beverly shook her head. "It's missing something. Like...something 'me.'"

"Let's reframe it around a place where people gather to gossip. Like...what about The Water Cooler?"

"Negative connotation."

Quinn hummed as she thought. "Or...The Front Porch?"

"I like that, but it's still not personal enough.

Using Apple Hill was a cute idea, but would it implicate you girls as cowriters?" Beverly laughed lightly.

"Wait a minute! That's it!" Quinn squealed.

"What?"

"You write from home. About what you see from your vantage point." Quinn pointed to the end of the cul-de-sac. "As a widow and a mother and someone in mourning but someone who...people around here *know*. You're a trusted source of info, and people need to believe that you aren't airing their dirty laundry. You're just talking about what's going on in town. People's business is safe with you...but you're also willing to talk about the hard stuff we deal with around here."

"Yoo-hoo!"

Quinn and Beverly turned to see Annette walking over with a familiar woman. As they neared, Quinn recalled who it was. The woman who'd be moving into the Best house, although her name escaped Quinn in that moment.

"Ladies," Annette declared. "I want you to meet your future next-door neighbor."

Quinn flashed a smile. "Hi. I'm Quinn." She gestured behind herself toward her house. "I live in—"

The newcomer cut her off. "The old Carlson

house." She beamed. "I've heard crazy rumors about that place."

Quinn blinked three times. "Oh, well. Right."

"I'm Elora," the woman said. "I guess I'll be right here." She gave a nervous laugh and shook Quinn's hand over her extended belly.

"Congratulations," Quinn replied. "Twins, I hear? How exciting."

Elora babbled on. "It's not in vitro." She laughed. "Everyone asks that. As if twins are a rarity in nature. Well, they *are*, of course. But this was all natural. You can ask Tad!"

An oversharer, Quinn realized. Not too dissimilar to Annette, really. She smiled.

Annette indicated Beverly. "And you probably know Beverly Castle."

Elora gave a nod, and Quinn steeled herself. Would Elora overstep her boundaries again? Ask about Tom and Kayla? Or what it was like to be a widow?

Thankfully, she didn't.

Beverly jutted a hand. "Hi, Elora," she said, her tone even and firm. "I live in—"

Again, though, Elora interrupted. "Oh, I know. You're that reporter. The one who lives in the house with the blue front door."

Beverly whipped her head to Quinn, whose eyes blazed with understanding. That was *it*. That would be Beverly's new column.

Beverly mouthed the title to Quinn, who grinned back. The House with the Blue Front Door.

CHAPTER 37—ANNETTE

The yard sale was, by all accounts, a success.

With Elijah and Vivi still whiling away in the backyard, Annette found a moment to sit on the front porch swing with Roman. He'd helped move the heavier stuff out to trucks and count change, but really, Annette had lately considered him to be little more than a ghost in their lives. Always in his office or on the phone, he was carrying their business, no doubt. But it was a lonely thing, to struggle like they had. To give up the Main Street digs and now the home where they'd raised Elijah.

Though Annette hadn't personally felt depressed, and Roman was mostly his usual even-tempered self, there was a tension in their marriage.

Like a weathered rope pulled too tight between a ship and its dock, ready to snap.

A nip was in the air. September had wound down. Annette thought about the Halloween decorations she'd packed. Would she still have energy to put them up once they were in the new house? Hopefully so.

"Whatcha thinking about?" Annette asked Roman, who was tugging the chain that connected the swing to the overhang.

"I'm thinking I wish we hadn't left this in escrow. It's a good swing."

She smiled. "Yeah. Well, we'll get a new one."

"With what money?"

Annette's chest tightened. "Things will pick up. It's a down market, Roman. That's not always the case. We knew real estate would be like this, right? Ups and downs. Downs and ups." She was echoing his words back to him. Words he'd used at the start of their marriage, when Roman's mother had suggested it was a dangerous idea to share a business with one's spouse. *What if the market ever tanks?* she had asked. Ever the optimist.

Roman had spat back that *Of course the market will tank! So what?*

She'd warned them that it would not only strain

their finances. So, too, would it strain their marriage.

At the time, young and stupid and full of hope, neither Annette nor Roman believed there'd come a day when they'd face such conflict. Where they were on the brink of falling out of love. Or, maybe more accurately, that they'd slip into a new norm of marital indifference. Where even financial woes didn't bring about arguments. They just brought about...placid change. The sort of change that they went along with out of pure survival mode.

But now, Roman's tone carried a bit of an edge. Like he wanted to pick a fight.

Maybe a fight could be a good thing for them. It could add some much-needed heat to an otherwise tepid relationship.

"Let's change our brand. That might help, right?"

"And what would we change? You always loved Best on the Block," he reminded her. "It was your idea!" His voice rose a note.

Annette shrank. "I *know*," she whined. "But...it's not working." This sort of admission came rarely from Annette's lips. She wasn't one to claim to be wrong. Ever.

Roman lifted his eyes to her. "And you think changing our whole company is the solution?"

"Maybe," she allowed. "I mean—moving is a

start, right? We'll reduce our bills and debt. So, that'll take the pressure off."

"But it won't fix the business."

"Then, I'll start showing again. You go back to the paperwork side of things, and let me show."

"I never wanted to show houses."

"You were better at it," she pointed out.

"Okay, well, then." Roman clapped his hands on the tops of his thighs. "What else? We change the name? Best on the Block is gone?"

Annette shrugged. "I haven't thought of a new name yet."

"Something simple? Like Best Realtors?"

"I think *Best* is the issue, maybe," Annette confessed. It was as much a confession to herself, anyway. She liked *Best*. She liked being a Best and she liked having a Best business. It was as much her identity as anything. But sometimes, who you were was the problem. This was starting to sink in.

Roman pushed up from the swing. "After the move, we'll start." He held out his hand. An olive branch, it appeared to her.

She slipped her palm into his. Maybe what they needed was a new view. A fresh start. On a new street.

In a house around the corner.

CHAPTER 38—VIVI

Vivi and Eli were nearly done with the fort. It had taken way longer than Mrs. Best had wanted—weeks instead of hours—but they got sidetracked easily. Either by silly conversations or the Carlson research project. Sometimes something as simple as a snack derailed the mission entirely.

But on that final Saturday of September, something stirred them to finish it. Maybe it was the fact that they had a different deadline—the research paper for Belinger's class.

Or maybe it was the fact that they *had* to, because come Monday, the house would no longer belong to the Best family. It'd belong to that *other* family. And God forbid Annette Best leave any trace of her humanity. She just wasn't the sort of woman. She was the clean sort. The orderly sort. Like Vivi's own mother, in fact. Not a germaphobe like Quinn, no, but Mrs. Best was her own brand of OCD. The sort who obsessed over her image.

Vivi could relate, actually, and so she didn't really mind it. First impressions, as Vivi knew all too well, could set the tone for the rest of a person's life. So Vivi wanted to help. She wanted to make 698 Apple Hill perfect for its new family. For her new neighbors. Especially that hot dad named Tad. Of course, Vivi's crush on Tad was just that. A crush. When it came to actual feelings, she was grappling with those elsewhere.

Eli ran the back of his arm along his forehead. Despite a bit of a chill in the air, he was sweating. Vivi was, too. At the small of her back and along her spine. Down her front and beneath the underwire of her bra. She wanted to remove her sweatshirt—Elijah's hoodie. But she'd much prefer to peel it off at home where she could wash it. Where he wouldn't smell any trappings of BO. Not that Vivi had BO. She snuck a whiff of her underarms. Her deodorant was holding up despite the sweat.

Sadie lay in a patch of sunlight nearby, alternating between snoring and startling in her dog-sleep. Vivi had never had a dog. Getting to know Sadie, though, had made her long for a farm full of animals of her own.

Every so often a little breeze wafted its way into the yard, tickling the wisps of blond hair at Vivi's neck, where they'd fallen out of her ponytail.

She reached for her water bottle, nestled among the debris of the structure they'd almost totally razed—Eli's word. Not Vivi's.

Eli picked up the pickax. They were down to the foundations now; only a few little gray blocks of it remained. The last thing to do would be to heft away the mess bit by bit in Eli's dad's pickup truck. Mrs. Best had given them money to use the county dump for this part of the job. Vivi hoped there'd be more to the pay than a pizza and a bottle of pop. After all, Vivi could use any extra cash toward Homecoming. Not that she had a date yet, but she hoped to go. And for the event, it'd be nice to have a brand-new dress and shoes. Maybe a manicure, if she could swing it. Asking her dad for money was a no-go ever since the summer incident. Now, Vivi was solely reliant on her own hard work and capacity to earn money. And if Mrs. Best couldn't cough it up, then Vivi would soon be applying somewhere in town. This was not an ideal thing, but it *was* an option.

Eli brought the pickax down on a chunk of concrete. It split into two and fell away, the pick moving easily into the soil below. But it stuck there. He gave the tool a jerk. But, again, it stayed stuck.

"How deep did your dad pour the cement?" Vivi asked.

Eli dropped to his knees and twisted both hands at the base of the pickax, tugging and jerking until it finally popped free. "Whew," he sputtered. "I'm starving. Should we stop for a break?"

Vivi nodded dramatically. "I'm famished." Sadie's ears perked up, and she hauled her body to all four feet, giving her coat a rippling shake and jogging over to where Eli and Vivi stood at the site of the old fort.

They played their "what should we get to eat game." She listed five options. He narrowed to three. She picked the one. As they playfully bickered back and forth—Eli couldn't get enough pizza, while Vivi wanted to lose two pounds and would prefer a salad from the market deli—Sadie pawed at the spot where the pickax had caught.

"Fine," Eli gave in at last. "*You* can get a salad from the market deli. I'll get a hoagie."

Vivi grinned and gave him a pretend sock to the shoulder. "See, Eli? It's all about compromise."

"Come on, girl." Eli whistled to get Sadie's attention as they made their way back to the house. But Sadie still hadn't obeyed by the time Vivi stepped into the house.

"Hang on," Eli grumbled and jogged out to the middle of the yard. As Vivi set about washing her hands, she kept her eye on him through the window. Eli was nothing like Dom, her ex. He was academic and bookish. He was thinner, but tall. He wore glasses and sometimes did quirky things like snap his fingers and adjust his socks in this super weird way. But he was nice. And she kind of liked his geekiness. It was...refreshing.

She finished washing up and returned to the door. Elijah had stopped trying to call Sadie in. He was now on his knees in the dirt, digging alongside her.

Bewildered, she swung open the door. "Eli! What's going on?"

He shouted back without twisting around. "Sadie found something!"

Turning irritable with hunger, Vivi stalked out across the grass and toward them.

"What?" It had better be something good. Like gold. Or buried cash.

Stopping at the soft hollow of earth, she leaned

over to get a better view then stood back up, sighing. "It's more concrete," she moaned.

"It's not concrete," he said. "It's like...wood or something."

Her interest was piqued, but only barely. "Wood? Like a subfloor or something?" Vivi had the right language but not always the right idea. Her dad was a contractor, but she never did pay close attention.

"Subfloor? No." He squinted close to the ground. "It looks like a...like a board, maybe?" Eli clawed in the damp soil, splattering Vivi's feet with the dregs of the earth beneath his childhood fort.

"Like a two-by-four?" She lowered beside him as he exhumed his discovery.

It was definitely not concrete. But neither was it wood.

Eli held the foot-long stretch of mottled, muddy ivory away from Sadie's whining.

Vivi whispered, her voice trembling and her feet shuffling backward fearfully. "Is that a—" her body convulsed.

Eli dropped the bone and caught Vivi before she tripped over the pickax. Righting her, he nodded slowly. "Yes."

Together, they looked back to where Sadie now dug maniacally, like a hungry mutt, scavenging for scraps, not like the well-groomed golden retriever she was. The purebred who belonged to a perfect little family and lived on a perfectly normal cul-de-sac in a perfectly safe town called Harbor Hills.

Vivi swallowed past a hard lump and squeezed Eli's hand. "Who do you think it is?"

But Eli fidgeted. He chewed the edge of his thumb, threw a glance over his shoulder and back at the house. At last, he shook his head. "I have no idea."

EPILOGUE

The girl, by now a young woman, never figured she'd wind up at Apple Hill Lane again. She'd sent that letter to Grandad mainly out of boredom. Partly of lonesomeness. *Not* out of an interest in revisiting the darkest days of her life, though.

But here she was, again at the top of the lane with no apple trees in sight. She made a mental note to ask about that. Who named that street, and *why*. What for? Not for apples.

Making her way from the street up to the door felt entirely different from the first time she'd walked that path. Grimier. Older. She took to the porch, weaving between boxes with black marker across them. She couldn't help but notice their labels. IRMA.

IRMA.

IRMA.

IRMA.

Nearly a dozen medium-sized boxes, each with IRMA printed neatly across the side.

She swallowed hard. Questions stirred to life in her head, and so did guilt, delayed and soft around the edges, but there all the same.

"It's you." His voice came from behind the screen door, croaky like he hadn't much used it. He sputtered a cough and the door creaked open. "Welcome home, Kid."

She set her jaw and frowned in spite of herself. "I can't stay."

"You got my letter."

"You need help?"

He winced. "It has to do with all that." He gestured vaguely outside of the house to the rest of the street.

She looked back, taking in the presence of the other homes for the first time in a very long while. All Carlson properties.

"We have to decide what we're going to do, you know."

"That's what your letter was about? Your plans for the houses?"

He waved away the idea as she slid past him and into the house. It was darker than she recalled. More crowded, too.

A shadow crossed down the hall, and the girl thought she smelled something cooking. "Is someone here, Grandad?"

"No, no. Not *exactly*."

She felt herself sway back.

He cleared his throat and followed her to where she stopped at the sofa. "Listen, I, uh...well...you see now, something *happened* in Detroit, and I had to... make a change. All right, now?"

She scrunched her forehead up. "Huh?"

"I needed your help to do away with something."

"Do away with something? Nana's stuff? In the boxes out there?" Confused, she indicated the porch.

"Oh, that's not it. I'll get the Penny House down to handle all that. It's another matter. It's, well, it's just that...it's Nana."

"What about her?" The girl's throat constricted instinctively. Despite the passage of years and the fact that the girl never cared much for the cold, old woman, guilt swelled behind her ribs, drumming her heart into a faster pace.

"Well, you see, it's that—" He cracked. His face, his body, and his voice. All of him split in half and he crumpled to the edge of his sitting chair where he buried his face in his hands and sobbed and sobbed.

"Grandad," she whispered, lowering to his side confused, terribly confused. "What is it? What happened?" But she knew what happened. Nana was sick something awful. She got worse. Grandad said so. They went to Detroit to see after some special treatment. It didn't work. She died.

She repeated all this back to him as if to ground them together over their shared history. Their family history.

His sobs turned to heavy breaths. "It wasn't that kind of sickness," Grandad struggled to whisper back, meeting the girl's gaze. "Nana didn't die of cancer or anything of the sort, Kid."

The girl shook her head. "Then how'd she die?" A sickening thought hit her like a punch to the windpipe, closing her throat and sending her inching away from the only family she had left to her name.

He stared past the girl and into the bowels of the house. Then he replied, but his voice fell so low and soft that the girl wasn't entirely sure what she heard or if she'd made the sentence up in her own head.

But the sentence hung there in the air all the same. "It was an accident."

That's when she knew that try as she might, she'd never leave Apple Hill. Not really. Not for good.

CONTINUE the saga with *The House Around the Corner*.

Head to elizabethbromke.com to join my newsletter and stay up to date with releases!

ALSO BY ELIZABETH BROMKE

Harbor Hills:

The House on Apple Hill Lane (1)

The House with the Blue Front Door (2)

The House around the Corner (3)

The House that Christmas Made (4)

Heirloom Island

Birch Harbor

Hickory Grove

Gull's Landing

Maplewood

Silent Mountain (S.E. Bromke)

ABOUT THE AUTHOR

Elizabeth Bromke writes women's fiction and contemporary romance. She lives in the northern mountains of Arizona with her husband, son, and their sweet dog, Winnie.

Learn more about the author by visiting her website at elizabethbromke.com.

ACKNOWLEDGMENTS

To all my wonderful editors: Elise Griffin, Beth Attwood, Tandy, Lisa, and Krissy—thank you for improving upon my stories. You are so critical to me!

My advance reader team and my readers: I am so lucky to have you. Your enthusiasm and support is the heart of my writing.

Mom, Dad—thank you for helping me get so far on my journey. Your encouragement has made all the difference.

Ed and Eddie, Winnie, too: May is almost here! The rest of our lives starts now! I love you!

Made in the USA
Middletown, DE
26 May 2021